THE SURVIVALIST SAGA CONTINUES

Once again it's proven that living a long life does not necessarily transition into living a happy life. Michael Rourke is angry, frustrated and scared, and has come to that point where he realizes that he has no way of protecting his family, much less his country, as President. He has information that he's up against an ages-old secret society bent on complete control of the entire world as well as the continued interference from Neo-Nazis, Aliens and, the Russians. Have I forgotten anyone? Oh, of course, scheming politicians. He could really use some advice from his dad, too.

With John Rourke still missing, Paul has taken on the role of family patriarch, working on setting up a new stronghold where hopefully the Rourkes and selected others can work together to take back the world and save it from destruction.

Sorrow is painful. Grief is debilitating. Sometimes a point is reached where even being a Rourke is not enough. Sarah has lost her husband, Wolfgang Mann, in a terrorist attack. Emma almost lost her older children as well as the other Rourke children at Camp Zero when they were attacked by juvenile kidnappers and murderers. Now, Emma mourns her baby, a tiny baby too weak to fight the virus that raced through his body. Why isn't her husband there to comfort her? Where is he? Is he still alive? She is slowly being shrouded in pain and uncertainty.

The Posse is committed to protecting the Rourkes as well as the loyal members of the Dog Soldiers but there are many more committed to their deaths.

Sharon Ahern

THE SURVIVALIST

#35

BLOOD MOON

SPEAKING VOLUMES, LLC
NAPLES, FLORIDA
2018

THE SURVIVALIST

#35 BLOOD MOON

Photo credit to Fantastic Caverns, page 111.

Editing assistance provided by Pamela Anderson and Steve Servello.

ISBN 978-1-62815-881-6

THE SURVIVALIST

#35

BLOOD MOON

Jerry Ahern
Sharon Ahern
Bob Anderson

To Jerry Ahern (born Jerome Morrell Ahern (June 23, 1946 – July 24, 2012). The father of John Thomas Rourke, his families, and friends and... enemies. A loving husband, father, grandfather, uncle and friend; he feared his God and not much else. He "planned ahead"—his goal was to resurrect The Survivalist Series; I hope he has smiled at these efforts.

The blood moon prophecy is a series of apocalyptic beliefs, which state that a tetrad (a series of four consecutive lunar eclipses, coinciding on Jewish Holidays, with six full moons in between, and no intervening partial lunar eclipses) is a sign of the end times as described in the Bible in the Book of Joel, Acts 2:20 and Revelation 6:12.

The idea of a "blood moon" serving as an omen of the coming of the end times comes from the Book of Joel, where it is written "The sun will turn into darkness, and the moon into blood, before the great and terrible day of the Lord comes."

This phrase is again mentioned by Saint Peter during Pentecost, as recorded in Acts, although Peter says that the date of Pentecost, not some future date, was the fulfillment of Joel's prophecy.

The blood moon also appears in the Book of Revelation chapter 6 verses 11–13, where verse 12 says, "And I beheld when he had opened the sixth seal, and, lo, there was a great earthquake; and the sun became black as sackcloth of hair, and the moon became as blood."

Once the warrior is no longer needed—once he becomes a relic of war—when it seems peace will prevail, he is mocked for being a savage, mocked for being a monster. But when America needed her Warriors to stand between her and doom, she called on her monsters to do what others would not. I say to you, you reading this, that the night is still cold, the danger still persists, and we who are your savages will again visit violence on those who would dare to cause harm to our land, not just for America but for our way of life, against all enemies, foreign and domestic, so help us God.

–Mariano Wecer,
Major, US Army Consultant at Asymmetric Warfare Group

"It takes smart men to win wars and it takes smarter men to prevent them."
–Frank Sullivan,
BG, PAANG (Ret) 2017

Prologue

General Rodney Thorne landed long enough to disembark Akiro Kuriname, and then climbed the cloaked Egg to a position of 40,000 feet above and oblique to the pyramid where he could observe the actions of the rescue element. As he ascended, he said, "God speed."

The four Vertical Take Off and Landing cargo planes beneath him belched out passengers that quickly set up security positions and moved on their assigned targets.

Halfway across the Pacific, the Operations Center went silent as four blips appeared above the Denali location. Operation Hay Stack was on, it had launched. Sullivan noticed it was strangely quiet. None of the surface ships were transmitting; neither were the submarines. He looked up at a technician.

"We still have communications?"

The technician checked all of the leads. "Yes Sir, just nothing coming in."

*****

Half a world away at the John Thomas Rourke Survival Academy's Camp Zero, the Rourke and Rubenstein children were trying to deal with the supposed accidental death of one of their classmates.

"This still doesn't explain the things that have been happening here," Natalie said.

"That's enough." Sandy Tempest, the instructor they called Ma, raised her hands, her sharp tone returning with a vengeance. She unclipped a walkie-talkie from her belt, but as she raised it there was a flash of movement from somewhere off to John's right, and then Ma staggered back.

John Michael's brain struggled to process what he had just seen. A tree limb seemed to have sprouted from Ma's chest… No, it was a crude spear. But why was it—? A scream went up and then the camp erupted into chaos. The other students scattered, crashing into one another in full panic mode.

Running for her life, Paula Rourke knew that she, and the other 'Rourke' children, could not remain at Camp Zero. To do so would be a death sentence. *I have to find the others,* she thought. With a start, she suddenly realized, *we can't trust anyone but ourselves. Why were we attacked? Who attacked us? Without knowing who and what had motivated the attack, it is impossible to determine the safest course. Assume the worst,* she thought. *Until we know differently, assume that we are being hunted and plan ahead.*

Chapter One

Eagles One and Two landed near their assigned entry point and disembarked personnel. Michael Rourke, dressed in a black battle uniform and covered in Arctic Extreme Cold Weather gear, led his Posse along the right side of the tunnel mouth. It was almost forty feet across and half that distance tall.

Akiro Kuriname had broken his Dog Soldiers into smaller teams, leaving one to "plug the hole" and provide rear security as the rest followed President Rourke and his Posse. Kuriname waited until the last man in the Posse was about twenty-five yards inside before he motioned for the Dog Soldiers to advance. He was distant enough that his people had a better chance to survive a surprise attack but close enough to provide quick back up fire power.

The tunnel mouth for the first fifty feet was weathered, looking more like the mouth of a cave rather than a tunnel. Coming out of a cliff face that had an overhang, the tunnel itself could not be seen from above. The counter-illuminated camouflage technology had made the tunnel mouth invisible from ground level. Michael wondered exactly how long this tunnel had existed, and then he decided he didn't want to know.

Ryan Fleming, the titular head of the POTUS Posse, held in his right hand his Lancer Model M1A1 .308 rifle with a casual confidence. For a man six feet nine inches tall, the feat required little effort. In his left hand was a device that tracked distance as well as magnetic orientation as they walked.

He had opened the zippered front of his parka exposing the crisscrossed bandoliers of 20-round magazines. The move also gave him access to his pistol belt from which an antique .45 Model 1911, a large bowie knife and a Lancer version of the old Ruger Redhawk .44 magnum.

"Sir," Fleming said after a while. "This tunnel is as straight as an engineer can draw a line with a ruler."

Michael Rourke nodded raising a closed fist to signal a halt. "How far do you figure we have walked?"

"Looks like about a mile and a half," Fleming answered. "We should be coming to something pretty quickly. Wish whatever is going to happen would kinda chivvy along, you know?"

Michael took a sip from his canteen. "Chivvy along..."

"Wish it would hurry up and get here. Not my cup of tea to wait on something."

"Yeah," Michael said, "I can see that. I can't say I like walking down this tunnel chute. We are wide open with no cover at all." He handed Fleming the canteen.

Fleming nodded taking the canteen. "As we say, 'Bob's your uncle.' That's it, nothing you can do about." He took a sip and passed the canteen back. "Might I make a suggestion, Sir?"

"What's that?" Michael asked as he replaced the canteen.

"How's about me and me troopers going ahead a ways? Kinda scout ahead so to speak."

Michael shook his head. "Thanks Ryan but we're looking for my father and I'm staying out in front. Now let's get moving."

*****

Why...do...your...people...come? The creature known as The Creator asked.

John Rourke examined the view screens and watched as the teams moved down the twin tunnels. *They have no cover at all, if the Aliens attack they don't have a chance,* he thought.

He saw two figures. One dressed in black carrying a CAR 15 and wearing two large single action revolvers, Michael. The other also dressed in black but with a sword strung across his back, Akiro Kuriname.

Rourke turned from the view screens. "They have come for me... not for you. You must not attack them, they won't stand a chance."

They... carry... weapons... they... are... armed.

"Yes, they are; they do not understand," Rourke said, pleading. "Let me talk to them, I can make them understand."

They... are... armed.

2

Rourke knew an armed attack would never work, he had to stop Michael and the others before The Creator did. "Please, let me speak to them. This is wrong; their deaths are not necessary." Rourke thought desperately. "It would not be correct, it would not be accurate!"

The creature stood impassive, the only movement was the head which periodically moved from side to side; on a human it could have been interpreted as quizzical or thoughtful.

Correct… accurate… must… be… correct… must… be… accurate.

John Rourke looked at The Creator and said, "There, that is my son... my offspring on the right and my good friend on the left. If you hurt them… if you attack them... I will kill you. Do you understand?"

The creature known as The Creator turned his head from side to side like a dog trying to understand a sound that was unfamiliar. Your... voice... is.... calm... I... sense... no... anger... in... you. I... believe... that... instead... of... anger... this.... is... what... your... people... call... resolve... commitment. I... believe... those... are... more... dangerous... than... anger... correct?

Rourke smiled. "Not only correct but accurate. We have made progress, you and I. Let us not throw that away needlessly."

The creature known as The Creator nodded. No… not... needlessly.

Then Rourke felt something, a "gentle probe" in his mind. He looked at the creature but the probe was not coming from it. Barely a whisper at first, less than an impression, more like a mental breeze, a thought began to form in John's mind. *Yes John, it is me…*

Chapter Two

Steven Delervello sat alone in his office staring out his single window. Outside, his "panoramic" view of the parking lot never failed to sadden him. Now, he looked at his wristwatch. He did not know it but in just a few minutes, the history of the world as he knew it was going to change.

*****

Dr. Jerome Morrell, professor of archaeology and an adjunct English instructor at the Mid-Wake Institute, tapped on the door frame of Delervello's office. He looked up and waved Morrell in. "Got a minute?" Morrell asked.

"Sure, what is on your mind?"

Morrell entered the office followed by a tall slender man. "Steve, this is a friend of mine."

Steve stood up, nervously looking around. "Otto Croenberg, I thought you were dead."

With a smile he said, "Obviously not. Have you had any contact with the President or John Rourke?"

Steve rubbed his right hand through his short, salt and pepper hair. "No, I'm getting a rumor that the mission to the Arctic was successful and John Rourke has been rescued but nothing solid."

Morrell and Croenberg took seats, and Morrell glanced at the mound of documents on Steve's desk. "Are you still trying to figure out whether or not the Third Chinese City is a legend or not?"

"Yeah, some reports lean toward it being a group of Taoist and Russians somewhere along the Sino-Russian border. Other reports hint that it is where Karamatsov's people that slept again after the surrender of the Russians are located." Morrell nodded without comment. "So, I ask again, what is on your mind?" Steve said.

Morrell looked down at his hands then looked up quickly. "We want to run something past you. You know how I am about conspiracies especially some of the more 'unconventional' theories..."

Delervello remained silent. Morrell stood up, closed the office door and began pacing as he talked. "I have been going over some reports. I know you are aware of this Peter Vale guy, the Neo-Nazi attacks in New Germany and Phillip Greene's activities. Well, I started running down some stuff on the VBB—the Very Bad Bug."

Croenberg leaned closer. "I fear, Dr. Delervello, the activities Dr. Morrell just identified are only the, as yet, unrecognizable tip of an iceberg."

I am amazed how similar Dr. Morrell's concept is to my own, Delervello thought.

"Herr Croenberg, forgive me but I am not a doctor of any field. Rather, my life's passion has been to know as much as I can about as many things as I can. That's my only qualifications for this position. I am exceedingly curious and blessed with a near photographic memory. But you two are talking about the Very Bad Bug that has been causing so many problems and deaths?"

Morrell nodded. "As a crypto-zoologist, I know this is a manmade creature; complicated manmade creature that required gene splicing and gene manipulation from at least three separate species of insects. Not many agencies have that kind of technology available here so I started looking overseas. New Germany has the technology but they are our best ally. The Russians have the technology, but I felt something was missing."

Delervello nodded. "Well, you have the KI, the Neo-Nazis and the Russians, take your pick."

Morrell shook his head. "Too obvious, too reasonable, I suspect there is some involvement with some, or all of them. But who is driving the operation, who is the brain behind it? It would take a lot of cash and a lot of intricate control to coordinate the VBB attack, the hit on New Germany that killed Wolfgang Mann, the attempt on Sarah Rourke-Mann and Emma Rourke, not to mention the ongoing disruptions against President Michael Rourke."

Delervello spoke quietly, "But you figured it out didn't you?"

Morrell's mustache moved as he smiled. "I think so. At least Herr Croenberg and I believe we are closer to the real issue than ever before."

Croenberg interjected, "Birth control. What do you know about birth control, not birth control by itself but as a method of population control?"

Delervello closed his eyes for a moment to gather his thoughts. "As with most things, it is difficult to determine exactly when and where our awareness of selective breeding began. It was however tied to heredity, inheriting traits from one's parents. Otherwise, why bother with improving the system if the system was working well enough naturally."

"Right," Morrell broke in. "But mankind wanted better crops, bigger bulls, small dogs... The list goes on."

Croenberg said, "Even in the days of Hippocrates and Aristotle, theories existed that were similar to Darwin's later ideas. Aristotle suggested that transmission of traits was transmitted through semen which interacted in the womb to direct an organism's early development. From the ancient Greeks through nearly all Western scholars through to the late 19th century, the inheritance of acquired characteristics was well established.

"Across the pages of time, the inheritance of positive attributes was recognized. Therefore it was also truth that the inheritance of 'negative' attributes was possible. The trick was to influence and encourage the former while discouraging the later. By the 18th century, plant and animal hybrid experimentation was going on. But it was for Gregor Mendel, a 19th century monk, to realize that inheritance patterns of certain traits in pea plants obeyed simple statistical rules with some traits being dominant and others being recessive. Charles Darwin would electrify the world with his theory of evolution by natural selection or survival of the strongest."

Morrell stopped pacing. "Right, but it was his cousin, Sir Francis Galton who worked out the idea of biological determinism. This was what the American Eugenics movement was rooted in. Eugenics, meaning 'well-born', was applied to a set of beliefs and practices that aimed at improving the genetic quality of the human race. The Eugenics movement's stated goal was to relieve human suffering by eliminating bad genetics. Well-funded and well-advertised,

6

Eugenics was practiced quite extensively in the United States many years before Hitler's Nazis developed programs in Germany."

Chapter Three

The park bench was occupied by a rumpled, elderly gentleman reading a newspaper. He wore a threadbare, brown wool suit. To a casual observer, he looked like an old Jewish grandfather or maybe a Rabbi. His name was Tuviah Friedman and he worked for an organization called the Aqrab. The word meant Scorpion and they hunt Nazis; more accurately Neo-Nazis.

"Here they come," a voice sounded in the ear wig microphone in Tuviah's right ear. He simply nodded once and rearranged the newspaper.

His partner, William Robert "Beaux Diddley" Delys, sat fifty feet away on another park bench. He pushed a baby buggy back and forth and sang a lullaby, a father stuck with getting his son or daughter to sleep.

Peter Vale and Phillip Greene approached from opposite sides of the park and stopped by the reflecting pool about four feet apart; neither looked at the other. Vale pulled a cell phone from his pocket and appeared to be talking on it. In fact, the phone was not turned on and his words were meant for Greene. "I understand that John Rourke has been rescued."

Greene gave a single nod. "But right now that is just a rumor… correct?"

"Well," Vale said into the phone, "the President and his father have not returned yet. However, I think it best that we plan on it being an actual event."

Greene gave another nod.

"Is your party ready to initiate our plan?"

Greene gave another nod and reached for a cell phone from his pocket, and said loud enough for Vale to hear, "The newly established Office of Special Records is now functional and we are mining information from every bank account, hospital record, credit transaction and government agency we have. All under the guise of track exposure to the VBB pandemic that has swept the country. Word has already gone out from the Center for Disease Control that a mutated virus is being spread by contact with the VBB and with its victims."

Vale smiled. "And since there is no cure for the virus, steps had to be taken to protect those that have not been exposed yet."

Greene nodded and spoke in the phone, "Isolation camps have been set up, 'patients' are being transported to them as we speak. It will be announced next week that 'in the interest of public safety' mandatory sterilization of those patients will begin. This is necessary to protect the unaffected population. Additional measures will be released and implemented over the next three weeks."

Vale turned to face Greene, still with his phone in his hand. "You have everything else on your checklists staged and ready for implementation?"

Greene looked at Vale and said, "Yes." Greene replaced the phone in his pocket, turned and walked away. Vale stood there for a moment making animated conversation for another minute or two before turning and leaving the park.

Tuviah Friedman stood and followed Vale. Walking with a cane and a limp, surprisingly the older man never lost sight of Vale.

"Beaux Diddley" Delys was about to stand and try to follow Greene when he noticed a man watching the crowd. The hair on the back of Delys' neck stood up but he did not know why. Delys stood, patted the bundle of blankets that covered the Omni-directional microphone and recorder that had captured the conversation, as he would a baby, and started in the direction of the man.

Close enough to get a good look at the man's face, he recognized him from a photo lineup Tim Shaw had shown him. Delys couldn't remember the name but he knew the face was that of a Neo-Nazi. The man stopped next to a park bench and pulled something out of his left jacket pocket, a flesh-colored surgical mask but Delys had seen this type before. On the inside of the cloth mask was a small filtration device that plugged the nose and allowed the wearer to breathe through the mouth piece. It was actually a small highly efficient and disposable gas mask.

Delys quickened his pace. The man pulled a dark cylinder from his right jacket pocket and reached with his other hand for the safety pin that would release the lever. Beau pulled a syringe from his pocket, jerked the cover from the needle and stabbed the man high in the shoulder at the juncture to his neck. A purified mixture of Ketamine and two other dissociative anesthetics hit the man's system like a bolt of electricity.

Beau bent and caught the dark cylinder with one hand, verified the safety pin was still in place and dropped the grenade into the baby buggy and said, "Excuse me, are you alright?"

He sat the now paralyzed man gently on the park bench. He sat down next to the man and acted as though they were in intense but friendly conversation. Activating the transmitter in his own ear wig, Delys spoke to Tuviah. "Tuviah, I'm still at the park. I lost Greene but I caught a guy about to bust some type of gas grenade right here in this crowd."

"Are you all right, my friend?"

"Yes, but we need to get this guy in custody before the syringe you wanted me to use on Greene wears off. Call Tim Shaw and have his guys show up in an ambulance, I'm going to fake him having a seizure. Hurry!"

Beau grabbed the man by the front of his jacket and laid him down on the bench. He shouted, "Doctor! Is anyone a Doctor? This man is having a seizure." A blonde nursing student with haunting eyes and a name tag that read "R. Moore" ran over and began to assess the "patient." It took less than twelve minutes for the ambulance to arrive and hustle the paralyzed man off to the Ambrose Federal Detention Center for interrogation when the Katamine cocktail wore off.

The ambulance driver got the nursing student's name for the report. She looked around for the man that had hollered for help, but William Robert "Beaux Diddley" Delys, Private Investigator from Baton Rouge and ex-HPD cop, had taken his baby buggy, recording equipment and the gas grenade and disappeared into the crowd before nursing student Rachel Moore realized he was gone.

Chapter Four

Morrell sat a tray with cups of coffee on the table, took one and motioned for the others to do the same. Then he sat down to continue. "It will probably be difficult for you to understand that the threat I'm trying to show you is as dangerous and diabolical as The Night of the War, Vladimir Karamatsov, Colonel Nehemiah Rozhdestvenskiy and all of the maniacs that John Rourke and his family fought for all of these years. Much like the plan to shoot the Eden Project shuttles out of the sky before they landed… what is happening now is a subtle attempt to dominate the minds and souls of mankind; and like Communism there would be only two classes of people, the haves and the have-nots."

Delervello made a note, "You're saying that under the guise of preserving and improving the dominant group in the population through population control, it is really nothing more than a plan for people control."

"Yes," Morrell replied. "It will create a second Holocaust that will make the first 'Final Solution' seem a timid affair. As the Nazis used political rhetoric to subjugate the European Jews before and during World War II, the Neo-Nazis will do the same thing; but instead of focusing on the Jews—which even today would be too blatant to succeed—they will turn on everyone other than Neo-Nazis and their supporters."

Croenberg nodded and spoke, "The Nazis and now the Neo-Nazis believe in the genetic superiority of Nordic, Germanic and Anglo-Saxon peoples. In every country they have control in they have implemented strict immigration and no cross breeding between the genetically superior and the genetically inferior. There has been forcible sterilization of the poor, disabled and 'immoral.'"

"Why haven't we heard about this?" Delervello asked with a frown.

"The Neo-Nazis have learned from the mistakes of their ancestors; they are more subtle now. They have developed the ability to hide in plain sight and get others to do their dirty work," Otto Croenberg said.

Morrell's lips turned up in a hard smirk. "Others… like the Progressives and even some of the weaker Representative party members. There are those intellectuals and academics that support the concept that 'the best blacks or the best browns or the best Asians are as good as the best whites.' They think about ten percent of all racial populations fall into the 'best' category and those should be allowed to mix."

"Excuse me but, Herr Croenberg, how did you learn so much about this program?" Delervello asked.

Croenberg stretched lazily. "During my recent 'other life,' remember I was the President of the German Republic for three consecutive terms and had started my fourth. A part of the foundation for my election platform had been a rather nationalist aspect of 'Rückkehr zum Vaterland,' or returning to the Fatherland. It was during the last election that I realized my country, my government, the Neo-Nazis, and a rather shadowy figure known as Peter Vale, were being manipulated like puppets. I followed several hunches and found that Mr. Peter Vale was the moving force behind your own Progressive Party... and they are also being manipulated like puppets."

"And then you were 'killed' in a car crash?"

Croenberg shook his head. "No, but it became imperative that it appeared as though I was killed in a car crash. Otherwise, I assure you... I would have been killed. Of that I have no question. I had learned too much... too much about something and several people have been spreading rumors for centuries but only that. No shred of fact and absolute knowledge has ever surfaced on this."

Delervello shook his head. "Are you saying that the Neo-Nazis, the Progressives, even Peter Vale are manipulated like puppets? So, who are the puppet masters?"

Morrell nodded. "And we have to find the puppet masters before it's too late."

Morrell stood and walked to the window looking out over the quiet campus, he turned to face the others. "We have learned that our own Center for Disease Control has amassed genetic information on our population. All of these ancestor search sites that can trace your linage have done the same thing; not just here but in every civilized country across the globe. Nothing like that has ever been accomplished by any political organization. Each citizen, by his or her own actions, simply placed their necks in the noose."

Delervello smirked and then frowned. "I can't believe this is going on right under our noses and no one has figured it out. How is that possible?"

"It was very simple, and very historic," Morrell replied. "You must remember this is not the first time this threat has reared its head. By 1910, a national Eugenics project was promoting Eugenic legislation. One was created just to 'investigate and report on heredity in the human race, and emphasize the value of superior blood and the menace to society of inferior blood.'

"At one point there were 376 separate university courses in some of the United States' leading schools, enrolling more than 20,000 students, which included Eugenics in the curriculum. All done under the guise of eliminating suffering and broken hearts by improving the citizens; there was to be no more insanity, no more Down Syndrome. The study of infant mortality resulted in investigating infant mortality rates in terms of genetics and promoted government intervention in attempts to promote the health of future citizens.

"It was the beginning of the American birth control movement, which saw birth control as a means to prevent unwanted children from being born into a disadvantaged life, sounds pretty innocent doesn't it?"

"Yeah," Delervello shook his head. "But I can see where you are going with this. How did you figure it out?"

"Michael Rourke..." Morrell said. "He came to me shortly after becoming president. Apparently there were rumors of something going on back then. But, it was the financial trail that broke the wall down for me. I could track who and what and when someone made contact with Peter Vale and how it affected something else happening in the Progressive political party.

"When the VBB epidemic struck, medical science was caught off guard. There had never been anything like this before. There was talk of sterilization of anyone that managed to survive to prevent passing on either the disease itself or associated mental disease or serious physical defects. All of this was of course, voluntary after all... 'It was individual women and not the state who should determine whether or not to have a child.'"

Croenberg spoke, "In other countries that have fallen under the Neo-Nazi influence it hasn't taken long for these programs to take hold and flourish. Political and social influence are used to help them implement these 'health' programs across the region; never associating the programs with the term Eugenics.

"I was unable to stop legislation that prevented mentally retarded men and women from reproducing and breeding more 'feebleminded' individuals. That type of legislation already exists in several countries overseas.

"Recently, the Central America Exposition opened in Costa Rica and will present new developments in science, agriculture, manufacturing and technology to include developments concerning health and disease, particularly the areas of tropical medicine. It is simply a subtle way to move toward 'race' betterment in areas of great poverty and disease."

"But, why now?" Delervello asked.

Morrell frowned, "Because it didn't just start. It isn't just now. Following The Night of the War, the few pockets of people that remained suffered greatly. As civilization struggled to crawl back out of the pit of World War III, something had to be done about the 'unfit.' Almost all pockets of humanity created prohibitions against marriage where one partner would have a disease such as epilepsy, or feeble-mindedness; up to and including forced or compulsory sterilization.

"Even after the worst was over and we began living as civilized people again, the burden of the 'unfit' was such that in many states the mentally retarded or those with low IQ were sterilized. Birth control became the new holocaust, facilitating the process of weeding out the *unfit*, of preventing the birth of *defectives* or of those *who will become* defectives."

Delervello shrugged. "Well, I can see how the wording could be offensive, but the process seems to have at least started out with the overall good in mind. How does all of this affect what is happening today?" He stopped for moment thinking and finally said, "So, who determines fitness or unfitness of someone?"

Chapter Five

Morrell slammed his open palm on Delervello's desk. "Exactly! The same person, people, group, agency or government that will determine who *is and is not defective*. Here is the bottom line... deep beneath the guise of protecting society and mankind from destroying itself through uncontrolled population is a simple goal—control. Control of the majority by a select minority and the stupid thing is the majority willingly gave that control to the minority.

"Seduction of the masses by a skillful public relations campaign geared to appeal to the development of women as more than mere birthers and the enticement of men to find more willing and liberated sexual partners. It was brilliant... brilliant but also diabolical."

"But that all took place before The Night of the War..." Delervello said, confused and more than a little apprehensive.

"Yes," Croenberg said. "And when the war came... the devastation was so great that the population of the world was nearly destroyed. If anything the concept of birth control would have spelled the death of the human race more certainly than the bombs. No one knows for sure how many humans actually survived The Night of the War, but estimates are pretty low; but not as low as forecasted.

"The 'reality' of nuclear war was not as bad as the 'imagining' of it. Mankind did not die out. The world was changed but not destroyed. We are now approaching the start of the anniversary, the 700th anniversary of The Night of the War and we are repeating the same insanities that destroyed the world in the first place.

"Bigotry did not die in the fires of the bombings; it did not die in the frozen winter that followed. Hatred and bias continue even today. Fear of what is different from us has always been man's downfall. What is different must be contained... controlled. It must be segregated, monitored and managed, or..." He stopped.

"Or... it must be destroyed?" Delervello interrupted.

"Correct. While men and women can be brilliant, altruistic and artistic... mankind has always been fearful, selfish, brutal and controlling. However, fine and glorious the costumes we wear, however great the cathedrals and libraries we build... they are just a veneer to hide that which is most ugly about us."

"But, why is this coming about now? Delervello asked.

"Partly because it has been almost 700 years since the old world... the world of John Rourke and his family ended. In those days, a generation was usually considered as every twenty years. After the destruction, it took a while for life expectancy to climb back from 'you were old at twenty-five and dead usually by thirty-five.' In those days, a generation was considered to be about fourteen years.

"Now the population density is much higher, civilization has returned too and in some ways superseded the civilization that Rourke and his family knew. Therefore, it is simply time for those old dragons to rise back up out of the smoke and fog of the past and try again to rule mankind. The late 19th and early 20th century was when the seeds of all of this and Progressivism were planted. Now we are seeing a second harvest, with the Progressive Party as powerful as they have become... it is time again."

"But, if the Representative Party folds, there will be nothing to stop the Progressives. What then?" Delervello asked.

"There is an old saying," Morrell continued. "For every person that is drawn to my flag... I am made weaker. Mankind has never been saved by great armies but by great men and women. Armies are simply the last resort before defeat; they kill people and break things. Death becomes indiscriminant. As has happened so many times in our past, the time for individuals— not political parties, not armies, maybe not even nations— is upon us.

"In war, unconventional war especially, the small groups can wreak havoc on larger, better equipped groups. To win this, no, that is the wrong term. To survive this, we must get smaller, more mobile. We must raid, not conquer. We must be insurgents, not soldiers. We must focus on activities that coerce, disrupt or eventually eliminate or overthrow the might of larger, better financed forces. We must win the support of the people; we must be able to hide in plain sight until we are ready to fight in the darkest of nights. We must have a base to operate from that is as secure as we can make it."

Chapter Six

Dr. Daniel Gregg, head of Mid-Wake's Astrophysics Department, was ushered into General Frank Sullivan's office. Natalia Rourke was sitting on the couch; Sullivan behind his desk.

"General Sullivan, Madame First Lady. I have the report for you... Enhanced satellite surveillance photos from a mountainous region of Antarctica show what appears to be a ship similar to The Egg that General Thorne has been testing at the entrance of a cave system. I believe this is tied to the Tunguska Event."

Sullivan frowned. "The what?"

"The Tunguska Event was supposedly a large explosion that occurred near the Tunguska River in Siberia on 30 June 1908. The explosion over the sparsely populated Siberian region flattened 770 square miles of forest yet caused no known human casualties. The explosion has been attributed to the air burst of a meteoroid that disintegrated some three to six miles above the surface of the earth since no crater was found."

Sullivan slid his chair back from the desk. "You said 'was' and 'has been.' Why?"

"I'll come back to that in a moment. We also have satellite imagery of an area in Siberia that contains strange dome shaped objects or iron houses or cauldrons, half buried in the permafrost. Local legends tell of ancient demons of the tundra, or taiga, and an unknown illness which kills animals and people who stay there too long. The local tribes call the place 'Uliuiu Cherkechekh'—The valley of death."

"Radiation?"

Natalia spoke, "No General, my people were familiar with this area. There was something happening there, but to my knowledge we never found out what it was."

Craig added, "We have a report from the 20th Century by a Mikhail Koretsky that says, '... even a sharpened cold chisel will not mark the cauldrons' and he tried more than once. Now, back to the Tunguska blast; say instead of an air burst from a meteoroid as scientists have believed, the event involved a UFO that slammed into the atmosphere with enough force to simulate an air burst. We know from General Thorne's flight our own ship is capable of speeds that could do exactly that."

"But you said there was no crater," Sullivan stated.

"Correct, we believe the pilot regained control and landed the ship close to one of these unexplained cauldrons."

"Why would he land near them?"

"No idea."

Sullivan sat with his elbows on the chairs arms, his hands together and his fingertips touching. "What if... what if they were outposts of our Alien visitors that were abandoned long ago and eventually forgotten?"

"I am aware that there were secret Russian missions into the taiga to discover how to gain entrance to these cauldrons," Natalia added. "We found some artifacts but never gained entrance. Some of those artifacts remind me of what we found at Göbekli Tepe. I did hear rumors of extensive sightings of UFOs coming and going in that area."

Sullivan's jaws tightened, he remembered John Rourke telling him about the UFO piloted by the dead Alien that crashed in Canada, years before The Night of the War. "Secret missions known only to a very few... a few like Karamatsov and his followers? But these... cauldrons you called them, are in Siberia? Now you say we have a sighting in Antarctica that suggests 'final proof of secret technology' on the frozen continent," Sullivan said with a frown.

Craig nodded. "Yeah, but now we know that UFOs **do** exist and so do Aliens. Even today, Antarctica's wastelands remain extremely hostile to human life making research and exploration very difficult. Some researchers believe Antarctica contains the remains of an asteroid more than twice the size of the space rock that hit near the Yucatan Peninsula and wiped out the dinosaurs. If true, it could be the asteroid that caused the Permian-Triassic extinction event and killed 96 percent of Earth's sea creatures and up to 70 percent of the vertebrate organisms living on land.

"There is also what is called the 'Wilkes Land gravity anomaly.' Satellites have spotted gravitational changes which indicated the presence of a huge 'structure' sitting in the middle of a 300 mile wide impact crater. Even today we are not sure what is under the ice at the South Pole, but remember the Admiral Piri Reis map?"

"The map of the world supposedly compiled in 1513 from military intelligence by the Ottoman admiral and cartographer, Piri Reis?" Sullivan asked.

"Yes, that shows the western coasts of Europe and North Africa and the coast of Brazil, and shows the Antarctic coast without the ice cap." Craig continued, "But the map is believed to have been based on older maps from the Library at Alexandria that date to the fourth century, B.C. Older source documents could take the search even further into the past."

"Even to the time before the ice cap existed?" Natalia asked.

Craig smiled. "Exactly, you see the history of what we knew has been turned inside out and topsy-turvy by recent events. Ghosts and legends, fact and fiction are now swirling together; smoke and mist entwined. The two greatest myths of all times, Atlantis and Aliens... Well, not only have they been proven to be real, they have been proven to be irrevocably linked in a way no one ever suspected."

Natalia stood. "General I think it is time I returned to Göbekli Tepe. Would you be so kind as to make that happen?"

Sullivan frowned. "Ma'am, there is a lot of 'activity' going on right now as I am sure you are aware. I would feel better if we could delay that trip for a little while, at least until we get all of our 'chickens back in the coop,' if you know what I mean?"

"Of course, General, I think that is a good idea. After all this time Göbekli Tepe is not going anywhere," she said, laughing.

Chapter Seven

The Captain of the KI did not, in the conventional sense, have an ego. He truly felt that it was the destiny of the KI to regain their rightful place as the rulers of Earth. More accurately, he truly felt that it was his destiny to be the rightful ruler of Earth. To do so, he was willing to let this Russian share the glory as one of his underlings.

"And soon, my people will join you in this historic plan. Our peoples joined in friendship for all times." Colonel Mikhail Sergeyevich had smiled at the concept.

Unfortunately, Colonel Mikhail Sergeyevich did have an ego. Besides that, he was a truly duplicitous and evil bastard. The Colonel smiled and thought, *At least long enough for us to master your technology then we shall make slaves of you as well.*

The Captain drew himself to an erect posture and nodded. "With your assistance and training, you are helping my people improve their combat skills to the point our two forces will be unstoppable." The Captain allowed himself a small smile as he thought, *Until such time as we no longer require your assistance then you also shall fall under our domination.*

Colonel Sergeyevich raised his glass in a toast. "Long, long ago our illustrious leader, Vladimir Karamatsov, set in motion World War III. Mother Russia was to rise as the leader of the new world and would have, had it not been for Rourke." He spit the name out.

"Now all of these years later, generations have come and gone and now our vengeance is about to descend on John Thomas Rourke and his hellish family. If only Karamatsov could be here to see it. His death will finally be avenged."

The Captain returned the toast. "You knew this Karamatsov?"

"Oh, yes. I knew him well."

The Captain looked puzzled. "But how is that so? I thought all was destroyed in the Night of the War."

Sergeyevich smiled. "Oh, my Captain, much was destroyed but certainly not all."

Chapter Eight

"That is why we are here today talking to you," Morrell said.

"I don't understand?"

Croenberg asked, "You are familiar with a black hole, yes?"

Delervello nodded. "Of course, a region of space time with such strong gravity that nothing can escape from it... including light. It is a theory of general relativity, that they are caused by a sufficiently compact mass that it deforms space time to form a black hole."

Croenberg smiled. "Exactly, Dr. Morrell and I have been conducting our own investigation trying to determine who the puppet masters are. However, you could say that our results are simply a 'black hole.' In our case, however, the absolute 'lack' of information has pointed us in an unintended direction that seems incredibly viable."

Delervello shook his head. "I don't understand."

Croenberg got up and walked to the white board on Delervello's office wall and began drawing. "Most of the time in an investigation you are attempting to allow evidence to prove itself and identify the criminal. Correct?"

Croenberg nodded and stepped back from the board. A drawing of concentric circles was there. "Sometimes, however, it may be necessary as in the case of a black hole to reverse the process and allow the crime to prove the evidence. The 'evidence' of what causes a black hole is invisible so you must infer that something, somewhere, has created the phenomenon, correct?"

"Occam's razor?"

Croenberg smiled and quoted, "Occam's razor states that if there are two explanations for an occurrence, the simpler one is usually the best one." Or another way of saying it is that the more assumptions you have to make, the more unlikely an explanation is."

"I think I am beginning to understand," Delervello said. "So, since your investigation has not confirmed the identity of the puppet masters, you believe we must infer their existence and identities from a total 'lack' of evidence?"

Morrell smiled at Croenberg, saying, "I told you he would get it. Steve, Otto and I are too close to this. We are so close we can't see the forest for the trees."

Delervello nodded. "And you want me to put a fresh pair of eyes on the topic to see what you two are missing."

Croenberg erased his drawing and turned back to Steve. "However, Mr. Delervello... may I call you Steven?" Delervello nodded and noticed for the first time a rather large and pulsating vein on the right side of Croenburg's scalp. "Then Steven, I warn you. Should anyone stumble across your efforts... should anyone ever surmise you may be investigating... the same people that forced my supposed death will kill you without a moment's hesitation."

Croenberg glanced at his wrist watch, and then said to Morrell, "I'm afraid I must leave... that other appointment I mentioned to you, Dr. Morrell."

Morrell nodded then said to Delervello, "I think we should continue this conversation in a couple of days. Will you be available?"

Delervello nodded. "Certainly, I feel... no, I fear I have little choice in the matter."

Chapter Nine

The tunnel opened up into a circular area easily 300 feet in diameter. Directly in front of them Michael counted three doors easily twenty feet wide and tall. Along the walls were two more doors, twice as big as the other three plus twelve "personnel" sized doors.

"Well, that's bullocks," Fleming said scanning the doors. "No damn good at all. No way to tell where these doors lead to or what's behind 'em."

Fleming turned back and signaled for two men to advance. Neal James and Steve Vaughn knelt down next to Fleming. "Okay Mates, I want you two to wait here and watch. The President and I are going back a bit down the tunnel for some coordination. You see anything let us know."

*****

Michael, Fleming and Akiro huddled over a hand drawn sketch of the circular area ahead of them. Fleming said, "I think this whole thing is dodgy... there's something wrong or just plain 'off,' in one way or another. I'm thinking some of those doors are decoys, some kind of trap waiting to be sprung on us."

Michael frowned. "Maybe but I don't think so. When this place was constructed... one hell of a long time ago... they couldn't have known we would be coming. Remember, this location was only a rumor before The Night of the War."

Akiro frowned. "However, I think Mr. Fleming might be correct in his call for caution. We should proceed carefully."

"I agree," Michael said. "Akiro, you have the most men. Send a two man team to make a quick recon on the larger doors. I figure those are hangers or supply areas of some kind, probably not occupied all the time."

Fleming nodded. "Clear them first then focus on those areas where we might find your father or encounter the Aliens."

"Not only Aliens but also other clones; ones that will be hostile to us," Kuriname said. That was when the middle door hissed slightly and began moving upward.

Fleming shouted, "Steady, Chaps... Safeties off!"

John Thomas Rourke stepped through the door with his hands up, as naked as the day he was born.

Chapter Ten

Chief of Staff General Frank Sullivan and Tim Shaw agreed if Michael Rourke resigned his office, the resulting turmoil would keep the media focused on him and the Rourke family for months. The scrutiny would be such that there would not be a moment of privacy available. A great many 'moments of privacy' were going to be required to do what had to be done.

Sullivan realized that "someone" was going to have to stay behind in a position that could facilitate on-going, surreptitious support of the new Retreat and the personnel assigned there. Besides the Rourke family, there would be the thirty-four members of the 442nd, Wes Sanderson's unit of thirty-six Marines, and the twelve man POTUS posse; a total of just under a hundred people. Furthermore, absolute secrecy had to be maintained at all times.

From time to time, transportation of some of these personnel to other locations would be necessary. Medical treatment for some of these personnel was highly likely, even probable knowing the Rourkes.

Sullivan picked up the phone and dialed a number. "Yes Sir."

"Bring two cigars and a bottle and meet me on the patio, Harvey."

"We smoking or we drinking?"

"Both," Sullivan said, smiling.

Chapter Eleven

When Sullivan arrived, Command Sergeant Major Retired Harvey Bishop had two drinks poured and was standing with two cigars and a lighter ready.

"Harvey, it's getting time."

Bishop looked around the patio then asked, "Should we be having this conversation in the open, Sir?"

Sullivan shrugged, lit his cigar and passed the lighter back to Bishop. He sat down and reached for his drink. "Probably last time we can Harvey. Have you thought about our last conversation?"

"Yes, Sir."

"Well..."

"Well what, General?"

"Damn it Harvey, are you in or out?"

Bishop lit his cigar, grabbed his glass and sat down putting both feet up on the patio table and crossing his legs. "Permission to speak freely, Sir?"

Sullivan took a drag on the cigar. "Of course."

"Frank, you keep drifting back to this. Thought we had had the conversation settled months ago. If you're in... I'm in. So I wish you would drop this, 'cause you're making me nervous. Either your memory is getting bad or the situation is getting worse and either one makes me nervous and I don't like to be nervous. Makes me constipated."

"How long we been together Harvey?"

"Can't rightly say, General. Ever since I walked up to that guard post at Fort Apache, dragging a travois with you on it. You're not getting sentimental on me are you?"

"Harvey, when my wife, Baby Girl, died... well, you're the only one that kept me from eating my gun."

"Frank, you've saved my life more times than I can count and saved my soul at least twice that I can remember. What the hell is going on in your head?"

Sullivan took a drink, sat the glass down and stood up and puffed on the cigar two or three times. "Harvey, you and I have had good lives."

"Actually made something of ourselves, Sir."

Sullivan nodded. "But we took some lives..."

"We saved many more, Sir."

Sullivan nodded. "Made some mistakes..."

"Probably going to make some more."

"Last chance to pull out, Sergeant Major."

"Not likely, Sir."

Sullivan nodded, chugged the last of his drink, inhaled deeply on the cigar then crushed it out with his foot. "Alright then, cut whatever ties you need to cut, Harvey. You're going dark as of right now."

"And what about you, General?"

"I'm sticking around out here so I can funnel stuff to you and the Rourkes. We start using the drop boxes tomorrow." He pulled some papers from his pocket. "Here is the list of when to use each one. Here is the list of safe houses and caches for resupply. Here is a map of the fuel dumps that are still active on the mainland. By the way, this particularly is no longer in the Department of Defense archives. Seems it got purged during an update. I need you to get this information to John Rourke, or Michael or Paul Rubenstein, but only them. Then I need you to get back here. I'm going to need some back up and I only trust you."

Harvey Bishop continued to sip his Scotch. He took a puff off the cigar and exhaled through his nose. "General, you don't like to fish, do you?"

"Nope."

"Don't really like to play golf, either?"

"Nope."

"Don't really have any hobbies?"

"Nope."

Bishop nodded, took his feet off the table, drained his glass and stuck the cigar in his mouth. Walking off he mumbled, "Least we don't have anything to miss, do we?"

Sullivan smiled and said, "Nope."

Chapter Twelve

Michael whispered "Dad" and started forward. The huge hand of the six foot nine inch Fleming grabbed him by the shoulder, stopping him in his tracks.

"Hold it Mr. President. Let's move easy here and see what we've got."

"Michael," Rourke said. "It's good to see you, Son. Please tell your men to stand easy. Trust me; if one round is fired... none of us will survive."

No one moved. Fleming leaned over to Michael. "Can you confirm this is in fact your father?"

Michael stripped off his pistols, handing them to Kuriname along with his rifle. Stepping out into the center of the tunnel with his hands held high, he said, "I'm going to show you something and I want you to tell me where I got it... agreed?"

John Rourke nodded.

Slowly Michael turned to one side and pointed at the huge sheathed blade on his belt. "Recognize this?" Michael asked.

"You were given it in Iceland by a sword maker whose name you were never able to pronounce. Satisfied?"

Fleming looked at Michael who nodded. "It's him."

Fleming said, "Why the dickens are ya naked, Dr. Rourke?"

John smiled. "Could not take a chance on itchy trigger fingers, had to have some way to shock you that would leave you hesitant and you wouldn't shoot. Figured hands up and butt naked would do that. Mind if I get dressed?"

Chapter Thirteen

Dressed again, Rourke stood with Michael and Akiro as Fleming rejoined the other men. Michael said, "Dad, we need to talk... some terrible things have happened while you've been gone."

Rourke looked down at his feet and deeply inhaled. Slowly, he emptied his lungs and looked at his son and nodded. "Go ahead, Michael."

Michael nodded. "There is no easy way to say this... No easy way and as you taught me..."

"Just tell me."

"Your baby was born, a boy. Emma named him Eddie after her brother; she said you two had agreed to that. Beautiful baby boy..." John frowned and motioned for Michael to continue. "Your son, Eddie died. The Hantavirus... that is what killed him. Those genetically modified insects you called the Very Bad Bug... well, we finally have them under control but not before there was an incredible loss of life."

"Emma?"

"Devastated, Mom is with her. Mom's not much better herself. Dad... Wolfgang Mann was killed in an attack on the New Germany Presidential Residence. Neo-Nazis were responsible; looks like the brothers of the guys that took Mom hostage... you called them 'Woody the Woodpecker' and 'Pocked Mark.' Their real names were Johann Burkholter and Franz Freed. Their brothers, Horst Burkholter and Helmut Freed, collaborated with a man called Peter Vale on the attack when Mom was taken and I suspect that Vale is tied into this attack also. For all intents and purposes, most of the New Germany government died in the attack.

"Several cargo vans, of different color and signage, were prepositioned near the Government Building six blocks away. Within each was a driver who triggered a rocket pod launcher that held nine 2.75 inch rockets, mounted to fire out a side door, and a .762 machine gun mounted on a tripod operated by a second shooter. Simply put, it was a slaughter. No one in Bellevue stood a chance."

Rourke turned, walked forward a few steps and stood with his back to Michael. After a few moments, he straightened and turned. "Funerals..."

Michael shook his head. "Already finished Dad. Paul and Otto really stepped up to the plate. After little Eddie's funeral, there was another attack, this time on Emma and Mom."

Rourke's head jerked up, his eyes hard; Michael shook his head. "They're alright. We lost a couple of Secret Service Agents but Mom and Emma did really well and Otto rescued them before either had a scratch." Michael stopped.

John looked at him. "What else..."

"Paul and I decided, in fact the whole family decided, it was time to put the kids in a safer place. We sent them to the Survival Academy's Camp Zero."

"That's the introductory level, right?"

"Right. We thought they would be safer and they could stand a change of scenery. They came back for Eddie's funeral; took a couple of days with the family and went back. There was an attack there. One of their classmates had died in a fall. The girl's name was Madison. One of the instructors, Sandy Tempest was going to send all of the kids back home because of the turmoil.

"In any event, Tempest was severely injured by a handmade spear thrown by an unknown individual. The camp erupted into chaos. We lost contact for several hours; John Paul was slightly injured in the fray. Our kids are alright; well... they are safe anyway. I don't know any of them will be alright again."

John shook his head. "Anything else..."

"On a better note, General Rodney Thorne figured out how to fly the captured UFO. The craft is able to connect with Thorne's mind. It was kind of quirky in the beginning but he was a fast learner. He was recently attacked by two unidentified craft that we now know are actually KI fighters."

Rourke turned his eyes hard. "Is Thorne okay, is he safe?"

"He's fine. He took both of them out."

Rourke was trying to process all of this information. "What about Manfred Schmidt, head of Wolf's security team? Any word on Willie Schultz, their chairman of Emergency Services and Conrad Lundeberg, the Federal Chancellor?"

"Schmidt is fine but the other two died with Wolf."

Michael quietly said, "That's enough for right now. There will be full brief-ings when we get back and you'll have the complete picture."

"The family is all at home waiting?"

Michael nodded, "Everyone except Paul. He is on a special mission that he and I cooked up."

"What?"

"Dad, I'm stepping out of the presidency. We have proof that Phillip Greene and Peter Vale have attacked everything and anyone associated with us. Vale masterminded the attack on Wolf. Paul is somewhere between Georgia and Missouri bringing equipment from the Retreat to a new one we are creating in Missouri. We are going underground, literally, and we will be doing it within days; at the most a couple of weeks. There is still a lot to do and more, so much more, I have to brief you on."

He stopped and reached inside a pouch on his belt and pulled a small leather wrapped package and handed it to his father.

John took it and unwrapped it. Inside was a polished doubled edged boot knife with a brown leather sheath and a green Micarta handle. On both the sheath and handle was the shield with his initials. Examining the blade, Rourke smiled. It read: A.G. RUSSELL STING on one side and The Survivalist on the other.

Michael smiled. "Thought you would appreciate that, I know you and Mr. Russell were friends. I had the Lancer Company put this together for your birthday as a surprise… but you weren't here for it."

Suddenly, the door to their left hissed and flew up.

Chapter Fourteen

A knock sounded at Delervello's office door. "Come in."

Jerome Morrell entered his office with three men he did not know. One was very short, the other two, six feet or better.

Morrell directed them to the couch and extra easy chair. "Steve, I wanted these men to hear your results. Let me introduce them to you. This big guy is William Robert Delys; he is a private investigator from Baton Rouge, and former Honolulu cop. He goes by the nickname of 'Beaux Diddley.'"

Delys–Diddley, nice touch," Delervello said, smiling.

Delys smiled and gave a quick nod.

"This gentleman is Tuviah Friedman." The little man smiled and pulled a small Meerschaum pipe already packed with tobacco and a lighter from his inside jacket pocket.

"Is it permitted?"

Delervello reached behind and unlocked and raised the window. "It is not, but we'll just keep it our secret.

The little man smiled. "I work for an agency called, the Aqrab. We are hunters, hunters of men and women, specifically Neo-Nazis. It was during the course of one of our investigations that I met these two gentlemen." He indicated Delys and the third man. I was hunting because he was a famous Neo-Nazi."

Delervello turned quickly to the third man and, then faced Morrell. Morrell smiled. The third man said, "Relax, Steven. All is well..." A life-like latex mask was removed and revealed Otto Croenberg.

Delervello's breathing had almost returned to normal, almost. "I've been living on eggshells since our last meeting. Jerome Morrell you almost scared me to death."

"I am sorry old friend but there was no safe way to warn you about Delys and Tuviah. Or, for that matter, that Otto would be disguised. Now, what have you found out?"

Delervello smiled. "Just as you suspected... nothing."

Tuviah Friedman's face contorted and he started to speak. Morrell held up his hand, "Hold it Mr. Friedman, and let him talk."

Looking at Friedman, Delervello said, "At our last meeting, we discussed the fact that finding anything out about these puppet masters would be virtually impossible. We decided the most important direction for this investigation to go was to learn... what we could not find out. In other words, the only evidence we would have is what was missing. Understand?"

Tuviah Friedman removed his hand from the pocket, bringing out a pipe lighter. Once the pipe was going to his satisfaction he said, "Most of the time, an investigator will find direct evidence, that is evidence that supports a fact without an inference. When direct evidence is missing or hidden you must go forward with circumstantial evidence. Correct?"

"Exactly, impressions about an event or events that someone did not see," Delervello said.

Croenberg added, "For example, if you went to bed at night and there was no snow on the ground but you awoke to snow, while you didn't actually see it snowing, you assume that it snowed while you slept."

Delervello said, "Exactly. How many of you have heard of the Rothschilds?" The Rothschild family was a wealthy family, thought in the years before The Night of the War to be part of a cabal.

"What is a cabal?" Delys asked.

Morrell responded, "A cabal is a group of people united together, to promote their private views or interests in an ideology, community, state, or business venture and they are not known to others outside their own small group."

Delervello continued, "The Rothschild family was one of several that were thought trying to institute a New World Order. From the 18th century they possessed the largest private fortune in the world, as well as the largest private fortune in, what at that time was modern world history. By the mid-20th century many politicians were using the term "New World Order" to describe the dramatic changes in political thought and in the new balance of power following the two World Wars."

Morrell stood up. "But it was the Progressives who welcomed these new international organizations and regimes in the aftermath of the two World Wars. It wasn't long before activists were pushing toward a 'real' New World Order."

Delys frowned. "How could something like that and the Rothschild family survive The Night of the War?"

"They didn't, or at least I don't think they did," Delervello said. "I have found no resurfacing of the families thought during the 20th century to be involved in the cabal. The Rothschilds, Rockefellers and the others all seem to have met destruction during or shortly after the atmosphere ignited following The Night of the War.

Chapter Fifteen

Bennett Arnold stood at the door with a drawn energy pistol. Ben Nehen and Steve Vaughn whirled, bringing their weapons on line. Arnold fired.

The blast blew Nehen and Vaughn across the room and slammed them against the wall. Almost in slow motion the two men slid down the wall, their clothes trailing smoke. "Freeze Dr. Rourke," Arnold said with a smile. "It seems that you and I are destined to have our paths cross, doesn't it?"

John Rourke smiled. "Well, at least for this one last time. I don't think we will be bothered with each other after today."

"Really and why is that, Dr. Rourke?"

"Because I'm going to kill you, you traitorous son-of-a-bitch," Rourke said with a smile as he swung his left arm up and dropped to one knee. Arnold's energy blast sizzled harmlessly over Rourke's head as the new Sting boot knife Michael had given him moments ago, flew like an arrow. Arnold tried to dodge the knife; it buried its point in his left carotid artery. The energy pistol clattered to the floor and bounced away from him as he reached for the knife.

"Wouldn't do that if I were you," John said, smiling.

Arnold jerked the knife out of his neck with a snarl, arterial spray splashed brightly in the harsh light. Arnold swayed then sat down quickly.

"The adult human heart pumps blood around several liters per minute under normal conditions," Rourke told him. "The adult human has about four or five, in some cases almost six liters of blood. With a severed carotid artery like you have, you are dying. Loss of blood pressure hits you first and you can't stand up."

Arnold hit the floor; he dropped the knife and grabbed at his throat to try to staunch the leaking blood. It didn't work.

"I figure forty-five seconds left."

Arnold dragged himself slowly toward the pistol laying several feet away across the floor. He started raising it when his eyes widened and glazed over as he passed out.

Then he died.

*****

The Creator stood in the third doorway, motionless, when Rourke stood up. Seeing him John turned to the others and shouted, "Stop, drop your weapons or we all die! This creature is not our enemy!"

The Creator raised his right hand; in it was the metal band that allowed him and Rourke to communicate. Rourke walked slowly toward The Creator and held his hand to receive the metal band and put it on his head as Nehen and Vaughn slowly stood up, stunned but apparently no other injuries.

Looking at The Creator, Rourke said, "I will translate for my people so they may understand you, agreed?"

Rourke relayed the message in the slow methodic manner he received it. Agreed... the... one... you... call... Arnold... acted... without... permission... Some... of... these... units... are... defective. They... are... unable... to... be... functional. They... are... broken... I... believe... it... is... because... the... parent... units... were... broken.

Akiro Kuriname, Ryan Fleming and Wes Sanderson approached Rourke and The Creator. Akiro came up to John, a broad smile on his face. "John, I am so glad you're okay."

"Akiro," John said shaking his hand and grabbing the smaller man in a bear hug. Just seeing Akiro energized Rourke. "I was just telling Michael how much I appreciate the quick rescue." Akiro looked at Michael and saw Michael make a quick shake of his head.

"Ah... of course my friend," Akiro smiled unsure what was going on.

For the next hour and ten minutes, they talked; Michael, Akiro, Sanders and Rourke plus the creature known only as The Creator and the men who had come to rescue John Rourke and, if necessary... kill The Creator. The last time a conversation such as this had taken place was before the Night of the War, almost 700 years in the past.

Rourke wondered if this one would come to a better end. *Could The Creator trust humans? Would the humans trust The Creator?*

Jerry Ahern, Sharon Ahern and Bob Anderson

It was a long hour and ten minutes, it was also the longest that Rourke had worn the metal band and the first time he had acted as a translator. He was tired when the experience finally ended.

Chapter Sixteen

Michael checked his wrist watch; it had been slightly over three hours since the rescuers had entered the tunnel. He had sent a runner back to the ships letting them know that his father had been successfully rescued and also to order that no word of that rescue should reach the outside world until they made it back to the ships.

Michael called over one of Akiro's Dog Soldiers, "Trooper, would you walk my father outside to the correct ship for me? I need to ask Akiro for a favor."

"Certainly, Mr. President, be happy to," Nehen said. "Come with me Dr. Rourke, it is good to see you again."

As they walked off Michael turned to Akiro and said, "I see you caught that also..."

"The part about the quick rescue?"

Michael nodded.

"Yeah, I caught it. Amnesia, some kind of memory loss...?"

"I don't know," Michael said. "Maybe sensory deprivation could be some kind of something that is easily explained. I sent word with the runner not to transmit that he had been rescued yet, so far only our ships know about it. I really don't want anyone knowing he's been rescued, not yet."

"Even your family?"

Michael nodded. "Especially to the family and make sure no one else does."

Akiro nodded, and tossed an, "As you wish," over his shoulder as he jogged ahead.

Michael pulled the radio from his harness and checked the screen, no service. As deep as they were underground, it didn't surprise him. He pulled the secure satellite phone from his pocket and checked it, same thing. Michael looked ahead, only about forty feet to the tunnel entrance, he slowed his pace.

Once he was out of the tunnel, he shouted ahead to Nehen, "Thanks Ben, have Dad wait at the ramp for me! I have to return this call!"

Nehen waved acknowledgement, shook John Rourke's hand and headed over to his own transport. Michael finished a short phone call and walked toward his father.

John smiled, "Everything okay?"

"Yes, just making arrangements. I want to stop off a Mid-Wake and let the medical personnel give you a quick once over just to make sure you're okay."

"Makes sense but let's make it quick. I'm ready to get home to the family."

*****

Michael checked his watch, and shook his father's shoulder. John Rourke was instantly awake. "It's okay, dad. We're about thirty minutes from landing."

John yawned. "Must have dozed off, don't know how that happened."

"You've been through a lot. First stop is going to be the hospital; I want you examined from top to bottom. As soon as we have a clean bill of health on you, we'll send word to the family that you're safe and Tim Shaw will escort you home. You can take care of Emma and have some alone time. Your kids are staying at my house tonight. Mom is staying with Annie. Natalia and I will see you tomorrow."

John smiled. "It's good to be going home, son. Even with all the terrible things that have happened. You and Paul have had a lot on you. You've done a really good job."

"It's good to have you back, Dad. I was afraid we'd never find you. To-morrow or the next day, we'll talk and I'll fill in the blanks for you. That's enough for right now. There's been a lot going on but you'll get full briefings in a couple of days that will give the complete picture."

John looked at his son. "Are you alright?"

Michael smirked, "NO... No, I'm not. I feel like a failure... everything... none of the things I tried to do as President... nothing matters anymore."

Chapter Seventeen

Paul Rubenstein pulled the truck to the side of the road. He pulled the curtain that separated the cab from the sleeping compartment and shook Haskins awake. "Yeah... yeah, I'm up. What's wrong?"

"Nothing," Paul said. "I just need a break from driving this truck. Help me off load the Harley."

Haskins grinned as he crawled out of the compartment. "Ready for some bugs in your teeth, huh?"

Paul nodded. "Yep, this truck is killing me. Weather's good so you spell me for a while behind the wheel and I'll scout ahead." It took just a few minutes to roll the Harley Fat Boy down its ramp, double check the fuel and oil and tires. Paul went back to the cab to get his Schmeisser and the musette bag containing spare magazines. After adjusting his shoulder rig for the Browning High Power, the Harley roared to life. "I'll make sure the way is clear and wait on you about ten miles up the road."

Haskins waved and climbed into the truck cab and adjusted the seat to fit his longer frame. Looking around he mumbled, "Now what did I do with it..." Popping open the glove box he found the old Marty Robbins eight track and popped it in the player. A little scratchy with age, he could still make out words from Mr. Shorty.

"The .44 spoke and it said lead and smoke... and seventeen inches of flame..."

Grinding the gears, Haskins check the side mirrors and pulled back on the highway. The sky was clear. "A good day to be alive," Haskins decided.

*****

Paul down shifted and leaned into the curve before accelerating out into the straight away. The rumble of the big Harley engine sounded good. *It's been too long since I've done this,* he thought. How far had he and John Rourke travelled on two wheels back in the beginning... He laughed out loud and shouted to the wind, "Who knows and who cares..." He down shifted and twisted the throttle, and the big motorcycle surged forward.

Paul smiled broadly and with his left hand shoved his wire framed glasses back up on his nose while keeping the throttle open with his right hand. That was when the bug hit his front teeth at over sixty miles an hour.

Chapter Eighteen

Tuviah Friedman frowned. "Then if there is nothing that you have found... why are we here?"

"I didn't say I found nothing," Delervello said. "I did not find what I was looking for, so I started looking for something else. Jerome Morrell mentioned birth control in our last meeting, especially birth control as a way for controlling the populace. If you can successfully control a populace, it is only a series of small steps before you can implement a New World Order.

"Next, since I found no evidence that any of the great, wealthy families of the 20th Century are still in existence, I looked for great wealthy families of our time. After identifying some fourteen families that are the richest in our world, I tallied up their combined wealth. In measuring against the world's financial holdings, net worth of individual citizens and the gross domestic product, or GDP, per capita... I saw something was missing.

"Further investigation showed travel links between forty-seven individuals who had absolutely no other linkages. These links show repeated travel on the same days with return dates for the last seventeen years. I took a chance and ran the same reports on these individuals' parents and grandparents..."

"And..." Friedman said.

"And, I found the same links going back three generations in the same families. Then I ran a series of exclusion algorithms against the populations of the U.S., Britain, Spain, New Germany, Australia, the German Republic and all other civilized countries."

"And..."

"And, the people you are looking for, the people that head this multi-cultural, multi-nation organization are Roderick and Andrea van Arnstein. Further, from their bios and physical stats, I would say both are the products of Eugenics enhancements and manipulation. Both are over six feet tall, the man taller by an inch. Physically, they are either perfect, or nearly perfect, physical specimens."

Morrell frowned. "I am surprised they are that visible."

"They aren't," said Delervello. "I can find nothing on either one of them after the ages of eighteen and sixteen. Since I could find no obituaries either, I make the assumption they dropped out of sight in order to stay off the public scene and out of the public eye."

Croenberg asked, "Who are they? Where are they? I mean, where is their base of operations... their headquarters?"

"They are brother and sister, the only two offsprings of a marriage between their father Helmut van Arnstein, a German Jewish banker, and their mother Claudine Benoit, a French scientist. Interestingly, their grandfather was also a German Jewish banker and his wife was also a French national. Currently, Roderick and Andrea are listed as German citizens, with German passports and other papers but they are living in Nancy, France. It is in the Lorraine region of eastern France about one hundred seven-five miles from Paris. It is a small metropolitan area with about just over four hundred thousand inhabitants of which one hundred thousand or so live in the city proper."

"Fascinating," Otto said slipping the latex mask back on, touching up the makeup and checking the results in a small mirror he placed in his vest pocket. "I was just thinking this morning I was feeling the need to travel back to the continent. Good day, Gentlemen."

"Hang on Mr. Croenberg," Delys said. "I'm going with you. I'm itching to see some new places myself."

Friedman was also standing. "Please include me in your plans Herr Croenberg. I have come too far to lose out now."

Chapter Nineteen

John Thomas Rourke walked slowly down the ramp of the VTOL craft. Stopping momentarily he grabbed the hand rail. As he steadied himself, he looked across the panorama of the scene unfolding around him. Mid-Wake, still as amazing as the first time he had been inside the gigantic domed city. "Hmmm," he said aloud. Rourke glanced over his shoulder at his escort and smiled, "Hmmm... I guess just 'Hmmm, it is over' or 'Hmmm, I'm free' or 'Hmmm, and I'm going home.' Frankly, I'm not sure. I guess a little of all three. Mostly, I'm glad to be going home."

Nehen nodded. "I understand Sir."

John Thomas Rourke felt great to be alive and to be free. He shouted to several of the Dog Soldiers that had just rescued him, "Guys, I want to thank you! I was afraid I'd never see the light of day again," as he and Michael walked to the ambulance that would take them to the hospital.

Michael's expression shifted as though a dark cloud had passed across his face. "Yeah, home... Dad, after you were taken prisoner..." Michael had practiced this speech a hundred times in the hopes he would find his father. Now, his mind was blank.

"What is it, Michael?"

Michael put his arm around his father's shoulder and simply said, "Let's get you settled in at the hospital and get those tests out of the way. There are some more things I have to brief you on."

Chapter Twenty

Sergeant Haskins, Paul Rubenstein's back up driver sat in the truck cab just off of what had been Kentucky State Highway 1354. The windows were down in the cab and Haskins was enjoying the breeze while he waited for Paul to return and lead them to the Dorena-Hickman Toll Ferry. It was the only remaining riverboat ferry crossing the Mississippi between Missouri and Kentucky and probably the only one left functioning in the United States.

If they could make the crossing and get to Dorena, MO, the rest of the trip would be just a little over three hundred miles and should only take eight to ten hours; if everything went alright. So far, Haskins reasoned the trip had been long but the only problem they had run into had been in the mountains when they were jumped a few hours ago.

Haskins realized he was tired, too tired. Unfortunately he did not make that realization until he felt the cold steel of a long Bowie style knife touch the soft skin under his neck. He froze.

"Dis look like 'im?" A tall skinny man dressed in buckskin breeches and a tattered flannel shirt said as he pulled Haskins face around.

"How the hell do I know? I didn't see 'em any more dan you did." The second man was shorter, not much over five foot four and heavier. One eye was grey with a cataract and when he leaned in for a closer look at Haskins' face, his breath made Haskins gag.

The tall man frowned. "You tha ones that kilt our kin?"

Haskins swallowed, the edge of the knife slicing the skin over his Adam's Apple. He decided shaking his head, no, was not a good idea. "Nope, I'm just passing through. Not from these parts, don't know anybody around here and sure have not killed anyone around here."

"How 'bout back in the mountains, few hours ago. Were dat you'ens?"

Crap, Haskins thought. *Did they track us all this way? I never saw or heard a vehicle.* "Nope, I haven't killed anyone. If you were following a trail, they must be ahead of us."

The tall one smiled. "Ain't been followin' ya. Been waitin' on ya. My uncle told me on the radio that a rig like dis un got into a scrap wid my cousins. Cousins got kilt, rig headed my way... you da first and only rig to get here. Gots to be ya."

With surprising strength for such a lean man, he grabbed Haskins by the nape of his neck and with one hand pulled him half way out of the truck window. "Uncle said dars two of ya. Whar's the other 'un."

"Don't know anything about anyone else, I just got tired and was resting. I'm by myself."

"Liar." The tall man slammed Haskins' head against the cab of the truck and Haskins slid to the ground unconscious.

Chapter Twenty-One

Paris, France bore little resemblance to its 20th Century self, Beaux Delys decided. Once the most populous city in France with almost two million citizens, it now boasts less than one million. Less than twenty square miles were the official administrative-limits as compared to forty one square miles back then.

Paris had once been famous for its museums and architectural landmarks. The Louvre was gone along with the Eiffel Tower and the Notre Dame Cathedral and the Gothic royal chapel of Sainte-Chappelle. The Arc de Triomphe had been rebuilt out of its own debris, but the damage to the stone structure was obvious.

Before The Night of the War, Paris was often referred to as The City of Lights—*La Ville Lumière*—both because of its leading role during the Age of Enlightenment, and more literally because Paris was one of the first European cities to adopt gas street lighting. In the 1860s, the boulevards and streets of Paris had been illuminated by 56,000 gas lamps.

Once hosting four separate airports, Paris today now could barely justify two. What was left of the Charles de Gaulle Airport was used mainly for merchandise and material shipments. The only available passenger flights came and went from Paris–Le Bourget Airport, almost seven miles north-northeast of Paris.

Delys decided that what was left of Paris reminded him of the old Humphrey Bogart movie, Casablanca. *Story of my life,* he thought. *If I owned a nightclub and IF I met one of my old flames, she would be married and the bad guys would be after her husband and I would get him out of town, but she would go with him... here's looking at you, kid...* Delys smiled. "Don't play it again, Sam. I can't take any more."

For some reason, probably because his last name was Delys and he was from Baton Rouge, Louisiana, Croenberg had decided he could speak French. He couldn't, he had trouble with Cajun English sometimes. However, somehow he had successfully rented a vehicle for the trip to Nancy. And for some other reason, probably because he was the youngest member of the little entourage, he also got stuck hauling the luggage to the vehicle.

They stopped at Reims, France for gas and a bathroom break. Beaux folded the map and said, "Not quite halfway, fellas. Next stop Nancy. Before The Night of the War, Nancy was only three hundred and fifty kilometers from Paris. With the new road construction, it's just under four hundred kilometers."

Nancy sat on the left bank of the river Meurthe, which was good because the bridges across the river were closed due to repair. Something no one in Paris had bothered to tell them. They checked into a hotel in the oldest part of Nancy, the quarter Vieille Ville – Léopold. It wasn't really a room, more of a hovel. But it was warm and dry.

Chapter Twenty-Two

On the way to the hospital, Michael smiled. "We have been worrying about the same thing but from the aspect of never seeing or finding you again."

"How did you find me so quickly?"

Michael turned to face his father. "What do you mean, Dad?"

"How did you find me so quickly?" Rourke said. "Did you track me from Mount Rushmore or what?"

Michael had a thought and asked, "How long do you think you were there?"

John Rourke shrugged. "Hard to be sure, nothing to judge passing time by; I guess a couple of weeks, maybe three..."

"Dad, you have been missing for almost six months..."

"Six months..." Rourke frowned and shook his head. "Michael, that's impossible. Maybe three or four weeks, unlikely... but I could give you that. Not six months, there's no way."

Michael frowned then smiled. "Dad, word of honor... six months. You have almost half a year to catch up on and some of it is not going to be pleasant, I'm afraid."

*****

Once John Rourke was settled in his hospital room, the taking of blood and urine samples began. During a break between testing cycles Michael said, "Dad, I've decided we're not headed home right away."

"Why not?" Rourke frowned.

"Honestly, there are a several reasons. First, we need to debrief you about your time with the Alien. It is imperative we learn some things as soon as we can, the first one being can we trust him or them. Second, I am concerned about the difference in time between how long you think you have been gone and how long you actually have been gone.

"Third, I need to finish briefing you on what has been going on since you were captured and what we found in the materials your expedition brought back from Mount Rushmore's Vault of Ages. Lastly, I need to let you know about something that Paul and I have been working on."

"Well, okay... we'll do it your way but I want to at least call Emma."

Michael shook his head. "Dad, I know you are anxious but I believe that once you hear me out you will agree that's not a good idea. There is too much at risk."

John Rourke took a deep breath, closed his eyes and exhaled slowly. "Alright Michael, we'll do this your way... for now. I will listen but I'm not making any promises."

"That is all I'm asking for right now; just listen and help me push through all of this stuff."

Chapter Twenty-Three

Paul had traveled a little ahead of Haskins; the lay of the land had required him to venture further than planned to clear several side roads.

My back hurts, and I've got to pee, Rubenstein realized as he slowed the motorcycle and pulled the bike to the side of the road at the base of a slight hill. He shoved the kick stand down and climbed off slowly. Stretching slowly to loosen his lower back up, he slung the Schmeisser over one shoulder, found a place to urinate and began walking slowly to the crest of the hill.

With a caution taught him long time ago by John Thomas Rourke, he peered over the rise. *Hmmmm, what has Haskins gotten himself into now?*

Wishing he had brought his binoculars from the Harley's saddlebags, he pushed his wire framed glasses up on his nose and squinted. A little over two hundred yards away, Paul could make out three people. One had a scoped rifle in his hands and was standing next to the truck and pointing it at someone lying very still on the ground. From the man's uniform pants and military t-shirt, he could tell it was Haskins.

The other had either a rifle or shotgun slung over his shoulder and was loosening the straps that covered the trailer for a look beneath. *Well, obviously they are not the welcome wagon folks.* Paul eased back down and ran to the Harley, popped open the left saddlebag and removed the Zeiss 10 x 40 binoculars he had liberated from the Retreat and moved back to the crest of the hill.

Crawling to lay in the tall grass, he kept a large tree behind him to hide his silhouette against the sky from those below. Slowly, he scanned the scene below for several minutes.

Appears to be only two, he thought as he saw Haskins move, then Haskins sat up and leaned against the front tire of the truck holding his head. *No good way to sneak up on them,* Paul realized. *With the exception of the small set of pines Haskins parked under for shade, there was no tree line available for a covert approach to the truck.*

Can't go charging down there, he reasoned. *They will have clear shots at me and could cap Haskins at any time.* He slowly backed away from the hill crest until he could stand, then stood and walked back to the Harley slowly; thinking. One thought kept bubbling to the surface of his mind. "He will win, who knows when to fight and when not to fight." John had forced him to read Sun Tzu's The Art of War the first time; Paul had studied it on his own after that.

Pushing his glasses back up on his nose with his left hand, he told the Harley, "Might not have to fight if I can get the drop on them. But I have to get close to them to do that; have got to be within fifty yards for my guns to have the range to take them down. The one with the scoped rifle could pick me off as soon as I top the hill, if he thinks I'm a threat."

The Harley did not answer.

"Wait a minute, let me think..." Paul remembered a time back when he and Rourke were trying to find Sarah. His Harley had started "coughing" and back firing through the carburetor, he was afraid it would quit running all together. He flagged Rourke down and under an over pass Rourke fixed it.

"All you have to do is richen the pilot jet and pull the mix screw out a couple turns," Rourke said. Of course Paul had no idea what he was talking about... or where the pilot jet and the mix screw even were located. But he learned...

Maybe, he thought. Just maybe... He dug out the Harley's toolkit and went to work.

Chapter Twenty-Four

Delys did not like Croenberg's plan. "We'll just walk around the first day like we are tourists. We'll ask a few questions and look around a lot."

"No one is going to tell us a damn thing. Not three Americans, well more or less Americans, walking around looking for somebody that is a local, maybe a friend even but certainly someone of importance."

Croenberg smiled. "Correct, they are not going to tell us anything. But they will tell someone that three Americans are looking for the van Arnsteins, and they will tell someone else and so on until someone tells the van Arnsteins."

Beaux saw the light. "Then the van Arnsteins will make contact with us, right?"

"Right, so we have to be ready at all times. Where are the special cases?"

"Right here." Beaux picked the three cases from behind the coach and laid the smallest one in front of Friedman. While the little man was opening his case, Croenberg had stripped to his underwear.

Beaux pulled the small Lancer Model 60 .38, their reproduction of the Smith and Wesson Police Chief and the Lancer PPK/S in 9mm, and its shoulder rig. He threaded the holster for the .38 so it would ride in the center of his back ready for a right handed draw. Beaux had worked with the rig so that if push came to shove, he could reach the little revolver with his left hand in an emergency. When he was satisfied, he put on the shoulder rig and checked both handguns before inserting them into their respective leather.

Tuviah dug out a snub, five shot .38 and stuck it in his right front pants pocket, a pocket he had had lined with thin glove leather. He put two Speed Loaders in his left lower jacket pocket and a switchblade knife in the back right hand pocket. Then he loaded his pipe with tobacco and touched a match to it.

Croenberg took longer to get ready. He buckled an upside down knife ankle holster on the inside of his left lower leg. He wiped the blade of a throwing knife and slid it into the holster. A heavy earth magnet held the blade securely enough that it took some effort to remove it. He put his pants and shoes on and tested the draw of the knife. Satisfied, he buckled on the metal and polymer sleeve holster rig and then put on the dress shirt. After buttoning the shirt, he shrugged and squeezed his right elbow to his side, activating a pressure switch.

The stainless Seecamp .32 automatic pistol slid silently and instantly into his hand. He verified the .32's chamber was loaded and locked the loaded magazine into the bottom of the grip.

Reaching into the bag, Croenberg withdrew a double Alessi shoulder rig with twin stainless Walther PPK .380 pistols. He slid the rig over his shoulders and shrugged them into position, then tested the draw for each pistol before returning them to the shoulder holster and snapping the trigger restraints. He put his suit coat on, drew in a deep breath and slowly let it out.

Delys turned to face Croenberg. "Otto, are you alright?"

Croenberg smiled. "I was just thinking... I knew for three years my time to leave my country was going to come. The party's leadership had determined that my leadership had 'moved the German Republic to a position of acceptance and responsibility on the world scene, but that position needed to be consolidated and pushed to the next level.'

"I just thought I knew who the players were. Now I found out that I did not. All I knew is what I had been allowed to see. I never conceived that the dogma would be so complicated and devious as it now seems to be. Duplicity, Beaux... duplicity...?"

"I don't understand?"

"Duplicity is defined as deceitfulness in speech or conduct. It can be speaking or acting in two different ways to different people concerning the same matter or double-dealing. Simply it is lacking in honor and truth. Life itself is difficult enough when people are being truthful. It is so much more difficult when truth is hidden, when people lie because they have neither the courage nor integrity to say, 'This is who I am. This is what I stand for.'"

"They are cowards," Delys said and turned away.

Croenberg turned. "Do what?"

Delys faced Croenberg. "Otto, people are cowards, everyone has something or someone they are afraid of. Everyone gets scared from time to time. No one wants to be punished for what they have done, or thought or said. That's normal... that's human. But cowards... well they are like traitors to a country."

Croenberg cleared his throat, "A nation can survive its fools, and even the ambitious. But it cannot survive treason from within. An enemy at the gates is less formidable, for he is known and carries his banner openly. But the traitor moves amongst those within the gate freely, his sly whispers rustling through all the alleys, heard in the very halls of government itself. For the traitor appears not a traitor; he speaks in accents familiar to his victims, and he wears their face and their arguments, he appeals to the baseness that lies deep in the hearts of all men. He rots the soul of a nation, he works secretly and unknown in the night to undermine the pillars of the city, he infects the body politics so that it can no longer resist. A murderer is less to fear."

"You are so right."

Croenberg gave a weak smile. "Not me; a Roman named Cicero."

"Damn, do you mean we had that problem way back then?" Delys shook his head. "You'd think by now we would have learned our lessons, wouldn't you?"

"But we have not, have we?" Tuviah asked as he puffed his pipe. "Now, are we ready to go, or do you two need more time to pontificate?"

Chapter Twenty-Five

Delervello and Morrell met alone this time and had talked through the evening, through the night and well into the morning. Morrell had said, "Well, I hope our friends are doing okay."

"I think they will be okay, I'm not too sure about us though," Delervello said, smiling. "So, you are saying we need a Sherwood Forest from which we can attack the Sheriff of Nottingham."

"Yes," Morrell said solemnly. "We need a Retreat from which 'we,' or more accurately... our forces, can go forth and do battle and then return to. We must help create separate individual pockets of resistance that can operate independently when necessary or cohesively when required. Mankind has always been both its own greatest danger and its only hope.

"Shakespeare said once that no man thinks himself a scoundrel. I don't agree. I have known many men that knew they were scoundrels, even bastards and just didn't care. If they would win the day, if they could get what they wanted at whatever price... as long as someone else paid the price... they would sacrifice their friends, their country, hell... even their God for power."

"But power is so fleeting. It never lasts," Delervello whispered.

"I did not say they were smart, just selfish and brutal and...," Morrell thought for a long time before saying, "and evil."

"So, you want to set up 'Tribes' like the Indians?" Delervello asked.

"Not exactly. Have you ever read Paul Rubenstein's Everyman Series?"

"Where he tells the story of the Rourke's adventures? Yes, some of it and some of those books written by... Jerry somebody, never can remember his name."

"Well, I think this next phase is going to be more like those stories. Small groups, maybe individuals on foot or maybe motorcycles... striking unexpectedly, doing as much damage as possible and disappearing to strike somewhere else.

Chapter Twenty-Six

The morning passed quickly, there simply was not a lot left of Nancy, France. The town itself had been originally founded about 800 BC they learned on a bronze plaque in the center of town. It had burned in 1218, been conquered twice, fought over at least five times... the worst was during World War II.

The Place Stanislas, a large pedestrian square, stood in the center of town. The square was a major project in urban planning, conceived by Stanislaus I of Poland as a way to link the medieval old town of Nancy and the "new" town built in the 17th century under Charles III, Duke of Lorraine. The square was also intended as a *place royale* to honor Stanisław's son-in-law, Louie IV.

The Place Stanislas was 125 meters long and 106 meters wide and paved with light ochre stones, with two lines of darker stones forming a diagonal cross motif. There were other notable buildings in the complex.

It was in the Opera House on the east end, that contact was made for the first time. Tuviah, from the start of the day had stood apart from Croenberg and Delys; they looked like they belonged together. Tuviah's small and somewhat twisted appearance did not match them; he saw the men approach first.

There were six of them, six Tuviah could see. He coughed loudly once and got Delys attention. Wiping his mouth with a handkerchief, Tuviah indicated the trouble approaching. Delys simply nodded and said something to Croenberg. They began walking toward the arc de triomphe that stood in the center of the fourth side of the Place. There was a double row of trees as its main axis.

Unobtrusively, Friedman peeled off, dropping back and scanning for more bad guys that might be approaching. He touched his left ear and turned on the small ear wig transmitter, "Looks like there are only six, copy?"

Delys said, "Yes, we copy. Let's see if we can take one of them alive."

Tuviah's harsh little laugh came across into Delys' ear, "Certainly, we will buy the winner supper tonight, no?"

Delys smiled. "Tuviah, be careful. Remember, you are not as young as you used to be."

"Ah, my big American... none of us are as young as we used to be or ever will be again. It is not youth that gives you an edge. It is knowledge and experience."

Delys turned to take a look over his shoulder at those approaching. When he turned back Otto Croenberg was nowhere to be seen. "Tuviah, do you see Croenberg. He's gone, I don't see him."

Tuviah spat on the ground. "Damn Nazi bastard. I should have shot him the first time I met him. Now it is two against six, those are not good odds. Be on alert Beaux. Two are breaking off and coming in my direction... that leaves four more coming toward you. Good luck my big American."

From behind one of the trees in the court yard, Delys said, "And to you, my little Jewish friend." He jerked the 9mm Lancer PPK/S from under his left arm and stepped around in front of the tree. He tried French first, "Bonjour mesamis." There was no response.

Okay, he thought, *maybe German,* "Hallo meine Freunde." Still no response, but the four men were drawing nearer. *When in doubt, try American,* he thought. "Hello my friends."

"Hello," came the response.

Beaux braced himself for action. "I seem to have lost my other friend. Perhaps you have seen him?"

"No, we will help you look." Two men peeled off in another direction and began searching.

In his ear, Tuviah said, "Better odds now, my big American... two coming for me and two coming for you. Much better, no?"

"Not much Tuviah." Delys made his move. He stepped quickly back behind the tree and shoved his right arm straight out. The Lancer PPK/S 9mm barked twice, one man dove for the cover of a large concrete planter, the other man staggered and dropped; his machine pistol clattered on the pavement.

The man behind the planter was taking slow, measured shots from the right side, with his pistol. *Sounds like a .45,* Delys thought, *but I can't be sure.* Delys couldn't get a shot from the angle he was in. *Gotta get him to expose himself.* Delys dumped an empty magazine and reloaded. He had noticed something. When he shot at the man from the left side of the tree, his opponent had to move further out to fire back.

Delys got set and fired three quick shots from the left side of the tree, jerked back and moved to the right side, held his breath and flashed his gun hand around the tree and fired twice. A scream, the clatter of another gun, and all was quiet.

By now Delys knew that the two who had gone for Tuviah must have made contact, but he had not heard anything. Had they already killed the little Jew? He also could hear the foot falls of the two that had gone searching for Croenberg running back toward him. He did a tactical reload, putting a full magazine in the PPK/S and drawing the .38 from behind him.

A string of 9mm slugs tore into the tree he was behind. He dropped down behind the tree and fired two rounds from the left side with the .38 then rolled to the right side and took aim with the Lancer. Two rounds... blam, blam... silence. Then he heard footsteps coming quickly toward him. He looked around the tree and fired at the approaching man. Blam, click...

What the... Delys jerked the 9mm back, *stove pipe,* the round had not completely ejected. He swept his left hand quickly over the top of the 9mm, knocking the problem round out and looked back. He was caught. The last man had him dead to rights. The muzzle of the machine pistol was unwavering on target and he, William Robert "Beaux Diddley" Delys, was the target.

Crap.

"Drop your weapon; drop both of your weapons." The voice was accented but Delys couldn't tell what the accent was. "Drop your weapons and slowly stand up." Delys had no choice.

He laid the guns on the ground and slowly pushed himself up. He raised his hands and slowly stepped around the tree. *This is probably when the son of a bitch shoots me in the face.*

"Blam..."

Chapter Twenty-Seven

Michael sat next to his father as the plane submerged and began sinking toward Mid-Wake. "It was shortly after the kids were rescued and Wolf was killed that I called a family meeting and broached the idea of sending all of the kids to the Survival Academy. Dad, I was the President of the entire damn country, and I was trying to figure out what the hell to do with my own kids. My own family!"

Rourke could feel his pain. "Being a dad is sometimes the most difficult, thankless job in the world."

"Yeah," Michael said slowly. "But no place was safe. John Paul was stabbed at the Academy. He's okay but it could have been a lot worse. Except for some emotional bumps and bruises, the rest of the kids are okay."

"What the hell happened?"

Michael shook his head. "We're not sure exactly what happened and we're not sure who is ultimately to blame. John Paul was stabbed, probably with his own knife during a fight with another kid at the Academy. There were other kids that called themselves Starlings. We're not sure if they are tied to the Neo-Nazis that attacked New Germany and killed Wolf or not.

"What we do know is they are trained assassins, kids trained to be assassins. They apparently killed several children that were on their way to the Academy and took their places in order to get closer to their target, a kid named Clayton Reynolds. His father is rich; he's the CEO of a leading energy weapons company. None of the Starlings survived the night, but there was little question they were part of a powerful entity with a global agenda."

"So... we don't think they were after our kids?"

"No, that is one thing we're pretty clear on."

Chapter Twenty-Eight

"Blam..." Delys flinched reflexively, he knew he was dead. His eyes slowly opened. *I don't hurt,* was his first thought.

The man dropped his machine pistol and grabbed his chest; blood was pumping out of him. He fell. Delys did not comprehend immediately what had happened. Tuviah spoke in his ear. "Well, my big American... we both survived, no?"

Delys turned and saw Tuviah and... and Otto Croenberg coming toward him. He sat down, took the extra rounds from his tactical reload and shoved them into the almost full magazine and shoved it back into the Lancer's magazine well. He replaced the rounds in the little .38 and shoved both back into their holsters. Then he walked over, confirmed the man that had just been shot was dead and collected his weapons.

Croenberg stopped behind the concrete planter, confirmed one man dead and confirmed his partner lying on the bloody pave stones was also dead.

Croenberg waved and the three began to run. "We have to get away before the Sûreté... the police arrive."

Chapter Twenty-Nine

"Michael, tell me more about Eddie," John said. "Do you have a picture of him?"

Michael nodded and pulled one from his billfold. "He got sick dad; Mom noticed he had a slight temperature and she and Emma kept checking it. When it reached 102 degrees they made contact with the doctor. Emma called her dad and the Secret Service car escorted them to the hospital running with lights and siren.

"When they got to the hospital, doctors and nurses rushed out from the emergency room area with a gurney and a nurse took Eddie from Emma. Tim Shaw got there about that time and followed the nurse inside.

"Mom called Paul to let him and Annie know they were at the hospital and to get the rest of the family up there as quickly as possible. Paul and Annie got there as quickly as they could but it wasn't long before Tim came back down and looked at Paul, shook his head and went back to be with his daughter."

*****

Russian Colonel, Mikhail Sergeyevich, stared at his own image in the full length mirror in his private quarters on the KI ship.

"You have done well Mikhail," he said to his image. "The events that Colonels Vladimir Karamatsov and Rozhdestvenskiy set in motion have been delayed too long. All this time since World War III, Mother Russia was to rise as the leader of the new world. And she would have if it had not been for that mudak, that bastard, John Thomas Rourke. Vladimir would laugh at how this game is going to end."

Chapter Thirty

Out of breath but also out of danger for the moment, Delys rasped, "Where the hell did you go Croenberg?"

Between wheezes, Tuviah said, "He came to save me."

Croenberg's breathing stabilized first. "When I saw two men were tracking Tuviah, I decided he needed more help than you did."

Tuviah smiled. "I am afraid my big American that I grossly misjudged this damn Nazi. They separated and approached from two sides. I took one with my knife, but the other one had the drop on me when I turned. I looked down his barrel and saw him smile as he squeezed the trigger. Suddenly there was a flash and I thought I had been shot. But there was no report, just a throwing knife sticking out of the man's larynx. He dropped the gun and fell back. That is when I saw Otto step out of his hiding place."

"We checked the bodies and came to help you," Croenberg said, smiling.

"Well next time, how about giving a guy a heads up when there is a change of plans. You know something as small as, "Oh, by the way... you're gonna be on your own for a while. I'm gonna go help somebody so don't count on me being here to back you up, but if I don't get killed I'll be back. You know, something kinda like that."

Chapter Thirty-One

Paul adjusted the sling of the Schmeisser so it hung behind his back and slightly to one side. He took off the shoulder holster, put it in a saddlebag and stuck the Browning High Power behind him, in his belt with the grip turned for a left hand draw. Then he put the battered field jacket back on and cranked the Harley.

It coughed.

*****

"Where's your pardna. I'm gonna axe you nice just one more time," the tall lean man said, waving his fist in Haskins' face.

"Told ya, I don't have a partner," Haskins said slowly. His forehead was bleeding but his nose hurt like hell. *Bastard broke my nose... again;* he thought and tried to figure a way out of this mess. He looked up.

Rubenstein's Harley was coming down from the top of the hill but something was wrong with it. Haskins could hear the motor coughing and thought he could see smoke trailing behind it. *Crap, he is going to walk right into this,* Haskins thought. *I can't even warn him.*

"Shorty, get ya butt behind the trailer. We got company comin'!" The tall man shouted then moved behind the truck.

Rubenstein's Harley sped up and slowed down, coughed several times and belched smoke several times from the top of the hill before dying. Paul waved and continued letting his momentum carry him down the hill, finally coasting to a stop thirty yards or so from the truck. Rubenstein put down the kick stand, shouting "You piece of crap!" and climbing off the motorcycle.

Walking slowly toward Haskins, Paul hollered, "Hey friend, can you lend me a hand? I've got some trouble with my motorcycle!"

Haskins smiled. *He knew; he has a plan. Hope to hell it works...* Haskins waved Paul closer but kept sitting. "Friend, I'd love to help but I've got problems of my own." The tall, lean man stepped from behind the truck and drew a bead on Paul.

"Stop where ya is, friend," he said. "Shorty, get out here."

Paul saw that the tall man carried a bolt action rifle and the other a sawed off pump shotgun with a pistol grip; there was the real danger. The bolt action would be slower to reload and fire again than the pump. Paul raised his hands slowly and turned slightly to keep the Schmeisser behind him. "Whoa, whoa... fellas I don't want any trouble. Just need some help with my ride and I'll be outta your hair."

"Shut up," the tall man said, walking toward the front of the truck.

Haskins looked at Paul and nodded. *Your play Boss.*

"Fellas, like I said. I don't want any trouble. Let me just mount up and I'll be out of here."

The man with the shotgun fired a shot into the ground. "You ain't going nowhere."

The tall man jumped and turned around. "Shorty, what the hell are ya doin'?"

Haskins and Rubenstein moved at the same minute. Haskins did a half-roll and swept the tall man's legs out from under him; the rifle went off and clattered to the ground as Haskins pounded the man's face.

Stunned, Shorty pointed the shotgun at Paul and shouted, "Freeze!"

Paul swung the Schmeisser up and said, "You freeze." That's when Shorty realized he hadn't worked the slide of the shotgun when he had fired his warning shot. Shorty was pretty quick, quicker than Paul had counted on. The slide jerked back, kicking out an old shell and forward, loading a fresh one. He fired.

Paul was already in motion, diving to the left as he squeezed the Schmeisser's trigger. A four round burst launched at Shorty. The first round hit in front of Shorty's feet, the second his right knee, the third missed him all together but the fourth drilled through his Adam's Apple, larynx and exited, forcing parts of his third and fourth cervical vertebrae to rip through his spinal column on their way out of the back of his neck.

Paul wheeled at the sound of the shot behind him.

"Freeze, sum bitch."

Rubenstein froze.

Haskins was down, blood soaking the ground under his chest. What looked like an old, cheap, snub nose revolver was smoking in the tall man's hand. "You kilt 'em, you kilt Shorty." The man's voice was a mixture of anger, disbelief and something else Rubenstein couldn't identify.

"Shorty tried to kill me," Rubenstein said carefully as he laid the Schmeisser on the ground, raised his hands and got to his knees.

"You kilt 'em, you kilt Shorty. Who are you people?"

Rubenstein glanced at Haskins, he had not moved. "We are just passing through here. We didn't want any trouble."

Keeping the revolver pointed at Rubenstein, the tall man walked toward Shorty and knelt. He leaned closer to look at the wound in Shorty's neck. "You kilt 'em, you kilt Shorty." Rubenstein could see the bloody froth moving around the wound. Shorty wasn't dead but he would be very soon. The tall man was focused on Shorty as Paul lowered his left hand, slid it under his field jacket and grasped the grip of the battered Browning and eased off the safety.

"You've killed my friend, I've killed yours. Haven't enough people died today?" Paul asked.

Shorty gave one final convulsion and the blood froth was still. The tall man reached up and gently closed Shorty's eyes. Paul realized what he had not been able to identify in the tall man's voice had been love.

The tall man said quietly, "No, not yet." He started to raise the revolver. Paul's left hand flashed out, the Hi Power belching fire and a 115 grain hollow point, quickly followed by three more. Two rounds tore through the man's heart; one blew an inch long section of the left collar bone out. The other missed.

The tall man fired twice himself, once at Paul... once at the sky, then lay still. Paul stood, pointed the Browning at the man's head and walked over, stepping on the man's gun hand and pinning it to the ground.

Paul stared and watched as the light slowly faded in the man's eyes. He retrieved the revolver, an ancient Röhm GmbH six shot .38 from before The Night of the War, simply referred to in those days as an RG. It amazed Paul that it had survived at all, they were known before the war as Saturday Night Specials.

Dropping the revolver in his jacket pocket, Paul picked up the Schmeisser and walked over to Haskins, knelt and felt for a pulse. Shaking his head, Paul felt for the man's dog tag chain, unsnapped the smaller chain and removed one of the two dog tags, dropping it in the pocket with the RG .38.

Thirty or so yards back in the woods, Paul found the two mules the pair had rode in on tied to a pine tree. He went through the saddlebags more out of curiosity than a desire to find anything and found pretty much what he expected... nothing of value. He loosened the cinches and dropped the saddles and saddle blankets on the ground. He untied the reins from one mule, removed the bridle and reins and swatted the mule on the rear. It walked off about 30 feet and began to graze. Paul set the other mule free, that one promptly galloped off and when the first mule realized he was alone, he looked around and went back to grazing.

Paul walked back to the truck and opened the door to the cab of the truck. Lying there on the console was a pack of Haskins cigarettes and his lighter. Paul pulled out a cigarette, lit it and sat leaning against the truck tire. He sat there thinking about his next move for a long time, long enough to smoke two more cigarettes before standing up and pulling a tarp from the cab of the truck.

He gently placed Haskins' body on it, wrapped the body and secured the folds with paracord. Paul had to move some of the cargo on the trailer to make a space for Haskins. "At least I can give you a decent burial with your friends," Paul said as he placed Haskins down and moved the cargo back to protect the body. Paul laid the Schmeisser and the Hi Power on a crate near him and lit another cigarette while he readjusted the pilot jet and the mix screw. Standing up he cranked the Harley and smiled: it ran like a top. He hit the kill switch; he dropped the ramps and eased the heavy Harley back up on the trailer, lashed the Harley to the trailer and replaced the ramps.

Opening the right saddlebag, he pulled a partial box of Federal 115 grain hollow points out. Dropping the Schmeisser's stick magazine he replaced the rounds he had fired from it first, making sure to slam the spine of the magazine into the palm of his left hand to set the shells correctly in the mag.

He popped the partial spent magazine out of the Hi Power and replaced it with a full mag. He repeated the reload on the partial spent mag and replaced the Hi Power and mag back into the battered shoulder holster and slung it into position. He shrugged slightly to settle it and put his field jacket back on. He dropped the partial box of Federals back into the saddlebag, latched the lid and hopped off the trailer.

Removing the bolt from the tall man's rifle and breaking the scope against the bumper of the truck, he dropped the rifle. He would drop the bolt along the road in a few miles. He examined Shorty's shotgun and decided to stick it in the truck cab. He fished around and found five rounds of buck shot in Shorty's jacket; he replaced the rounds Shorty had fired, did a final body check for ammo or weapons.

He looked around one last time and checked his watch and looked at the sky and frowned. *Crap,* he thought, off in the distance, in the direction he was headed; he saw heavy, dark clouds building. He checked his watch and determined he had at least one more night on the road before he would be at the Caverns.

Crap. Now my mouth tastes like crap after all those cigarettes. He dug around in the truck cab until he found the canteen. Taking a swig, he swished it around in his mouth and forcibly spat it out. *How can anything that feels so good taste so bad?*

Unslinging the Schmeisser, he laid it on the passenger seat. It was then that the circumstances really hit him. With Haskins dead, Paul was alone. He put Shorty's sawed off between the seat and the driver's door and cranked the truck. He pushed the clutch in and grabbed first gear. Easing the clutch out and turning the wheel, he headed back toward the road. Feeling a bump Paul looked in the mirror and realized his back tires had rolled over Shorty.

He grimaced and said, "Oops, sorry Shorty." He pulled onto the roadway and took one last glance backwards at the two bodies, lying where they had fallen.

Chapter Thirty-Two

Peter Vale smiled at Phillip Greene as Greene dabbed at the leaking spit that drooled from his lip. "The shell game is known by many names: Thimblerig, Three shells and a pea, and even The Old Army Game. It involves gambling, the winning of a prize. It involves a belief in one's own confidence to follow the pea and it involves a swindle.

"Most often there are several identical containers, like cups, shells or bottle caps, placed face-down on a surface. A small ball is placed beneath one of these containers so that it cannot be seen, and they are then shuffled by the operator in plain view. One or more players are invited to bet on which container holds the ball—typically, the operator offers to double the player's stake if they guess correctly. Where the game is played honestly, the operator can win if he shuffles the containers in a way which the player cannot follow. However, we have rigged the game."

"We're cheating," Greene said.

"So harsh..." Vale whimpered, then iron flashed in his voice. "You're damn right. We cheat because we have to win. And we are going to win. It is how we will bring down Michael Rourke's Representative Party. That game and our two secret weapons, one that was discovered just twenty-five years ago in the personal papers of a political firebrand from long ago.

"It is the only known remaining copy of what has been described as a 'treatise for taking over.' It was and is a play book on how to gain social, political, legal and economic power... and keep it. For those that believe in capitalism and freedom... it has been called the most 'damnable book ever written.'"

Vale had received the book in the mail from an unknown sender several years ago and had studied its concepts in fine detail, and by implementing them had amassed a sizable fortune and was about to destroy the American government and the Rourke family. Vale smiled. "It is not that the meek will inherit the earth or that the sheep can take over... but they can believe they have finally received the power and the blessings of that power."

"What is in the book?"

Vale smiled. "Snippets, just snippets, small truths that have tremendous effect when understood. Things like 'The power others think you have is more important than what you do have.' And "For ridicule there is no defense, its sheer irrationality makes it a potent weapon' and 'A threat of a thing happening is more impactful than it actually happening.'"

Greene frowned. "I don't understand."

"It's really simple, a person's imagination and ego can dream up far more consequences than I can. But my favorite is 'Push a lie hard enough and long enough and it will become truth, push a bad thing hard enough and long enough and the fools will decide it is a good thing.'"

"Is that how we defeat the Rourkes?"

Vale shook his head. "Partially, but we have to illuminate the target, in this case... the Rourkes. Then we polarize them, knock that hero image down and make the public believe the Rourkes are after them personally."

"How do we do that?"

"Our second secret weapon is terror; brutal, senseless, dramatic and suicidal terror. The most effective terror weapon is the individual suicidal shooter or bomber. Very nearly impossible to detect and virtually impossible to stop... All you need is a lunatic willing to blow themselves up or die killing a lot of people. And they are really not that hard to find. You simply look for losers, some minority or religious cult group that outsiders look down on and fear.

"The media is using craziness to explain crazy as relates to suicide bombers. Why did he blow himself up? Because he was crazy. How do you know he was crazy? Because he blew himself up.

"Some ask, how do we explain suicide bombing? You don't have to explain it, you simply use it. Instances of brutality and terror have periodically visited virtually every religion and ethnicity. Both the perpetrator and the victim suffer from it. The fascination and predisposition we have for inflicting brutality, the innovative effort dedicated to the task, and the visceral thrill of it... for some it is as good as sex, for others... it is better.

"You simply find someone who not only has no reason to live but is actively seeking a good reason to die. It is through their dying they see the purpose of their useless little lives. Then you use that person in the latest twist in a long line of socially-sanctioned brutality and rituals throughout history.

"Lump them together with an identity, a set of rules and most importantly... an enemy. Then you convince them that they are in possession of... not truth but THE truth and they truly will willingly spend themselves, their fortunes and their intellect because they are, 'on a mission from God.' And because it is now a society... you never run out of idiots who will to blow themselves up... Unless, of course, if you blow up the society, hahaha."

Greene thought for a moment and said, "And the media will spread the word, because it is news."

Chapter Thirty-Three

Before the Night of the War the Dorena-Hickman Toll Ferry had been the only operating ferry crossing the Mississippi River between Dorena, Missouri and Hickman, Kentucky. It only operated during daylight hours but it ran seven days a week year round except on Christmas Day. A ride on the ferry provided a unique opportunity to experience the wonder and beauty of the Mighty Mississippi. The Dorena-Hickman Toll Ferry could be accessed at the end of State Highway A near Dorena, MO or the Hickman Ferry Crossing off Kentucky State Highway 1354.

Back then what was basically a diesel powered river tug boat that moved a barge back and forth across the Mississippi for twenty dollars or so. It could safely handle vehicles up to seventy-five feet long and as heavy as 80,000 pounds. But that was a long time ago, in a different world.

Now the ferry was simply a barge pulled back and forth by a pulley system powered by a steam engine. The barge was able to take the truck and trailer but just barely. Once the wheels had been chocked to keep the rig from moving, the rear of the trailer extended two full feet past the end of the barge. Instead of the fifteen or so minutes in the old days, the trip now took a solid forty-five minutes.

Once on the Missouri side, Paul pulled off the barge and drove up to the highway and pulled over. After checking Haskins' body and the rest of the load, he checked his GPS. He wouldn't make it to the Caverns until tomorrow afternoon... He pulled off the road about fifteen miles later in the ruins of an abandoned pre-war town. There wasn't even a sign to tell him the name of it. After he set up the counter-illumination generators and made camp, he explored what was left of the town.

This was the first time in the trip he had been alone. While Haskins could be irritating at times and his sense of humor left much to be desired... he still had been company. Paul had set his rations on the still warm engine of the truck and by the time he returned—empty handed—it was ready to eat. The weather was pleasant, if a little chilly, and the sky was clear so Paul pulled out the collapsible hammock and his sleeping bag.

He dug out a bottle of Seagrams he had taken from the Retreat and Haskin's pack of smokes. He sat on his folding camp tool, sipping whiskey, smoking cigarettes and thinking about so many nights like this he had spent on the road with John Thomas Rourke so long ago.

He sat there for over an hour before the stress of the day and the exhaustion of his trip settled in on him and sleep claimed him.

Chapter Thirty-Four

The first bout of testing was over and the Rourkes were finally headed to Hawaii under fighter escort. "Mr. President..." Colonel Steve Johnson, the Air Force One's pilot said over the intercom, "Sir, we have a problem."

In the private conference room, Michael and John Rourke looked at each other. Michael punched the intercom button. "What kind of problem?"

The pilot hesitated, "Well, Sir... ah.... actually we have about three problems. We have lost contact with the other planes on this mission. We have the heaviest fog conditions I have ever seen and our instruments aren't functioning correctly. I've climbed to try and get out of this soup but it isn't working. I'm high enough we shouldn't collide with any of the other planes though."

Michael frowned. "Are we still over land?"

"Probably, Sir, but I'm just not sure. Wait a minute... Sir, the fog is dissipating. I can see a little better. There... it's gone. Holy crap..."

Michael keyed the intercom again. "What's the matter?"

"Sir, ah... we are alone up here. I don't see any of the other planes at all. They aren't on radar either. Sir, you better get up here."

Chapter Thirty-Five

"Air Force One, come in."

"Unknown station, this is Air Force One. Identify yourself."

"Air Force One, this is the New National Socialist Faction of the Democratic German Republic. You are instructed to land and surrender your ship and passengers."

Michael took the microphone from Colonel Johnson. "This is Air Force One and that is a negative. We will not land nor surrender our passengers."

The voice continued in a pleasant tone, "Good Morning Mr. President, I trust you are well and your mission was a success. Please convey to your father my congratulations on his rescue."

"Who am I speaking to?" Michael asked.

"Patience, Mr. President..."

Michael thought, *I know that voice... but who...* Vale, Peter Vale.

"We shall meet soon enough and all will be made clear to you. By the way, I bring you greetings from your stepfather, Wolfgang Mann."

Michael reached into the combat pouch on his gun belt and removed a transmitter/homing device and activated it. The device was supposed to be impossible to hack, trace or tap into... he hoped it was. "General Thorne, this is POTUS on Air Force One, come in. Over." He waited. "General Thorne, this is POTUS on Air Force One, come in. Over."

"Roger POTUS, this is Thorne. I have your position. Are you okay? Over." Thorne scanned the holographic screen, found the pip that blinked Air Force One and mentally commanded his craft to intercept it.

"Affirmative but need your assistance. We have been contacted by forces identifying themselves as the New National Socialist Faction of the Democratic German Republic. They have instructed us to land and surrender our ship and all personnel. Over."

"Roger, Air Force One. I have you on visual. You have bandits approaching from the west, I count... six. Repeat six bandits approaching from the west;

look like Russian MiGs. I will be in range shortly, what are you instructions? Over."

"General Thorne, would it be too much to ask that you splash those bandits. I'm instructing our pilot to take evasive actions."

"Roger that, Air Force One. No problem at all..." Thorne visualized his weapons display, selected Trickle and thought, *Trickle charge from the nose sweeping left to right at the targets.* Green lightening leapt from the nose of The Egg and smashed the six approaching MiGs; they never had a chance. Thorne hit the transmit button on his communication set, "There you go Air Force One."

Michael smiled. "Thanks General, we'll take it from here."

"Roger, POTUS, you're welcome, Sir. Thorne, out."

Ten minutes later, Michael was thrown to the flight deck by the impact of a missile. Colonel Johnson shouted, "We are hit and we're going down." The co-pilot was sending "Mayday, Mayday... this is Air Force One and we're going down."

Unfortunately the missile had destroyed the radio.

Chapter Thirty-Six

Sullivan was furious. "How the hell did this happen?"

"Fog of war, slipped through the cracks." The Air Operations Center Commander, Navy Captain Mitch Reynolds didn't take a step back from Sullivan's tirade. "Call it what you want... the issue is it has happened. President Rourke's plane had departed Mid-Wake. Shortly after they emerged from the ocean and were in flight, they were engaged by six MiGs. General Thorne destroyed the MiGs, but shortly after that, Air Force One disappeared."

"No radio message?"

Reynolds shook his head. "Nothing, they were continuing on toward Hawaii as planned. Heavy weather including a massive fog developed just before they were entering Hawaiian airspace. The other ships were tracking the President's bird and although the interference was making radio contact virtually impossible, the planes were maintaining a coordinated flight plan and good formation. That is until they came out of the fog bank and verified visually that Air Force One was in fact not in the formation."

Sullivan fumed, "Captain, are you telling me this was some kind of accident. A computer glitch and we have lost the President, his father and the people on the plane?"

Captain Reynolds shook his head. "No General, I am not... this, whatever the hell happened was a sophisticated, purposeful, electronic attack. Not only was Air Force One apparently disabled, the fact that it was disabled was hidden from the rest of the mission components. That involves a dynamic interception and manipulation of the avionics and communications systems. There are no world players we know of that are capable of that kind of interference, but these points are not what trouble me most."

Sullivan sat down heavily, a headache forming at the base of his skull. "Okay Captain Reynolds, I'll bite. What troubles you the most?"

"The weather, General; for this operation to have gone this smoothly... our opponents had to be able to control the weather."

Chapter Thirty-Seven

As the mental fog pushed back, John Rourke became aware he had settled the phone back into its cradle. He slowly removed his fingers that had tightly fisted themselves around the handset while the short conversation took place.

Slowly turning to his wife, Sarah, he half muttered, "I've got to go back. They need me to finish the job."

"John, you just got back. You haven't even spent 24 hours in this house, and a good bit of that time was taken up with you cleaning your guns and equipment. You can't go back. Tell them to get someone else to do their dirty work."

"I made up the plan and carried out my part of it. Evidently, the ones who came in to follow through failed. I have no choice but to see the mission accomplished. They're counting on me."

"They're counting on you! For what? Why you? Do you ever consider they are aware that you'll go anywhere, at any time, just to prove you can fix things? This is no more than some silly little mission that's a game of keep away. By the time anyone has whatever it is, no one will want it anymore."

"This is important, Sarah. There's a lot at stake."

Her heart pounding, Sarah tilted her head back, staring right into her husband's eyes. "Your family is important too. There's a lot at stake here. Can't you see that? Your son, your daughter, your wife—don't we count for anything?"

"You knew when we got married that this job would require some sacrifices," Rourke said, trying to keep his voice calm. "It didn't seem to bother you when you were working in hospitals—the long hours away from home. We didn't argue then."

Sarah walked across the room and rearranged the sketches she had been working on for a book project. She moved them across the oak table she used for laying out and compiling her sketches. Finally, she stacked them, one on top of each other, and then shoved them all aside, returning them to their original state of disarray. "We didn't have to argue because at least when I got home I knew you'd be there with me. Yes, sometimes you were gone, but at least I could work more hours at the hospital and then stay home when you were there. And, we didn't have children then! Children need a father! Now, you kiss us goodbye, walk out the door, and ride off into the sunset or whatever the hell."

"But it's not..."

"It is," Sarah's voice trembled. "You go off. We're here in the middle of nowhere, our mission to wait for your triumphant return."

"The middle of nowhere is our home. You like the farm. You've always said how good it was for the kids to have the space to run, play..."

*****

Rourke woke up then sat up. *There is smoke... no fire, not yet,* he thought. *Michael, where's Michael?* He tried to stand but couldn't. *Have to find Michael.* A groan came from his left and a section of aluminum bulkhead began to rise then fall away revealing his son. A deep cut ran across his forehead, stopping just before it transected his left eye. Blood ran down his face and it took a moment for his eyes to focus.

"You okay?"

Michael nodded, touched his hand to his face and saw blood on his fingers. Gently tracing the cut with one finger, he smiled a crooked smile. "Boy, that's gonna leave a scar."

John smiled. "Help me up. We have to get everyone out of here."

Chapter Thirty-Eight

The landing had been a hard one; the VTOL would never lift off under its own power again. However, the ship seemed to have saved most of its crew and passengers; at least for the present. As the inhabitants walked and crawled from the wreckage, from off in the distance came the sound of vehicles approaching. Akiro Kuriname shouted orders and a defensive parameter hastily formed.

At the crest of a rise 500 yards from the wreckage, a line of vehicles appeared. Kuriname had been specific in his instructions, "Be ready to fight for your lives, but don't show yourself until the signal."

For almost two minutes, Horst Burkholter the younger brother of Johann Burkholter and Franz Freed the older brother of Helmut Freed, surveyed the wreckage through binoculars. Helmut let his binoculars drop to the floor; he stood and made a circular motion with his arm then a downward slash with his hand. "Down," he shouted. "Down, find the Rourkes. Leave no other man alive but bring the Rourkes to me."

Then like a wave they came over the crest of the rise to smash into the steel and lead of the defenders of Air Force One.

*****

The distance was closing quickly and Freed and Burkholter were almost giddy with bloodlust. Twenty all-terrain vehicles with a driver and a gunner apiece threw dirt and debris as they raced forward.

"The Neo-Nazi force has fast vehicles. They are both well-armed and well supplied," Ryan Fleming smiled. "Things could not be better for us."

Akiro Kuriname smiled. "I am interested in hearing your logic for such a statement Mr. Fleming."

Neal James popped off, "No sweat Mr. Moto; my main man Fleming has a plan. You are going to love it too, I'll bet." James looked back over to Fleming, "Ah... you do have a plan, right?"

Fleming smiled. "Absolutely, the Neo-Nazis are vicious and brutal, no argument there. They are also well supplied, but here's the deal. They have never encountered opponents like us; they are used to attacking soft targets with little or no opposition. Schools, churches, synagogues... gun free zones where they know will not have any opposition. Additionally, they are so well supplied that I doubt they have ever walked more than a mile during any operation and certainly not in austere and dangerously situations.

"First thing we do is disable their vehicles and put them on foot in these hills and mountains. Being on foot is going to cut down on the amount of supplies each man will have; ammo, water... heavy things like that."

Neal James laughed. "I bet they don't have tents or cooking gear. No need for them to have them. Not with their supply system. Once you take their strengths and turn them against them... we have victory."

Kuriname gave a small bow. "Another student of Sun Tzu, I see."

James smiled and then frowned. "Who?"

Chapter Thirty-Nine

Earl Burger closed the bolt on his .50 caliber sniper rifle and squeezed the trigger. The .50 caliber heavy sniper rifle ripped through the engine compartment and struck the gas tank. The resulting explosion sent shrapnel that took out the nearest ATV, the driver's head pulverized upon impact with a flying battery from the first.

Shots from the defenders had been focused on the driver and or the tires of the approaching ATVs. Earl Burger and Steve Vaughn's heavy rifles were stopping the ATVs and dropping Neo-Nazis at significant ranges. Too far distant for their rounds to even threaten the men huddled around the wrecked VTOL carrier plane. As Fleming had anticipated, these punks had never before had significant resistance to contend with.

The battle was short but vicious and Fleming's plan had worked. Within a few minutes almost all of the vehicles had been either wrecked or couldn't move because of the damage. The attackers ran, running for their lives toward the left flank. Many but not all made it.

Fleming said, "Now, we are going for the maximum amount of casualties in the shortest period of time with no losses to our side." He knelt down and pointed across the valley. He picked up a small stick and started drawing in the dirt. "Vaughn, I want you and some of Sanderson's people to set up an L formation with machine guns along the bottom of the L and your assaulting position at the side. I want Listening/Observation Posts, on either side of the ambush element to alert us to the enemy approaching the kill zone and to provide security.

"Burger, I want the claymore antipersonnel mines with your assault force. When the enemy enters the kill zone, initiate an ambush with the Claymores. I want the machine guns to run for a 'mad minute' then cease fire while you guys charge through the kill zone.

"Jim Judy will set up the second ambush here, right along the escape route we left open to the enemy. The bad guys will run head long into a cross fire from Judy's hidden team firing straight ahead and Burger's chase team firing at the oblique. Bingo, we now have the maximum amount of casualties in the shortest period of time with zero losses for our side.

"Spivey... Michael Spivey!" Fleming shouted. Spivey came running.

"Yes, Ryan."

"I want you and Neal James to scour this wrecked ship and see if any of our AATTVs survived and see if Neal's motorcycle made it. Report back to me in the next few minutes and let me know."

Spivey nodded and jogged over to Neal James. "Come on, Neal."

"Sparks." Fleming waved at Patrick Haryett. "Get on the radio. See if you can put it back together. We have to get communications working." Turning to David Lynn, "David, find your field kit and work with Chief Sanderson's medics to set up a triage center... I want to see if any of the enemy survived and can be patched up for interrogation. Get with Dr. Rourke, he can be a big help both with the triage and the interrogations."

Chapter Forty

The first assault had been disastrous for Burkholter and Freed. Over half of their raiders had not survived. Broken and burning ATVs lay scattered across the field below. They decided to split what remained of their force with the idea to surround the wreck site, "like the horns of a bull." Freed explained he had heard about the way Genghis Khan had fought and always liked the idea. There were two problems: they had fewer men left than the force they were facing and they had only eight vehicles left.

Four vehicles tore off down the western slope and the four others attacked from the east.

Rourke watched and counted the number of men approaching from each side and shook his head.

Damn amateurs. He thought, *You are going to get all of your men killed.* He lit a thin cigar with the battered Zippo and exhaled the smoke through his nostrils.

"Akiro, you cover the west side, Sanderson you get the east. The VTOL's crew, Michael, his Posse and I will hold the center. If you can catch one of the folks alive that would be best; don't put your men at risk to do it however. Understood?" Both acknowledged with a nod and moved to set up a battle line.

John quickly checked the Detonics and satisfied they carried full loads shoved them into the double Alessi shoulder holster. He dropped the 30-round mag from the CAR 15, tested the spring to be sure it was likewise full, rammed the magazine back up the mag well, popped the release as the bolt flew forward, ripping the top round out of the mag.

Michael still carried his CAR 15 with a bandoleer of magazines, the two almost matching .44 single actions. Each of the VTOL's carried the military's standard issue 9mm pistols; the chief pilot had a short version of Lancer's full size M4-A23 carbine in .556.

Akiro's team opened up first with rifle fire. Ryan J. Fleming, Posse Team Leader, saw the trouble before anyone else did. "They were trying to outflank us." He grabbed Steve Vaughn's shoulder, "You're with me!" he shouted at

David Lynn and Earl Burger. With hand signals he instructed to back up Akiro with precision rifle fire and Burger to do the same with Sanderson's Marines.

Lynn flopped down next to Akiro with the modified sniper rifle and fired two quick shots. Akiro shouted, "You missed." Lynn smiled and pointed, two of the advancing vehicles were belching smoke, fire erupting around the engine compartment.

"No I didn't, Sir, just put them on foot where they are easier to hit." He fired three more rounds and reloaded. With ten slugs he had dispatched two vehicles and eight men.

On the other side, Burger pulled his 7.62x51 G113 and buckled on the 25mm grenade launcher with its changeable five-round revolving mag and opened fire. He decimated two vehicles immediately with three rounds. He opened up with the 7.62 tumblers and started chewing the hill side. Someone screamed behind him and saw one of Sanderson's men had been hit in the face; blood, bone and gray matter spewing from the back of his skull.

Another Marine stood up, his body jerking from the impact of a half dozen rounds. Burger looked back and saw the shooter behind a boulder. He drew a bead and waited. He saw the barrel of the shooter's rifle began to peek around the corner of the boulder. *Patience,* he thought, *be patient.*

Blam!

His rifle kicked from the recoil. Burger reacquired the boulder in his telescopic sight. Nothing. Burger looked up to be sure he had the right boulder, and then panned the scope and stopped at the edge of the boulder. *I couldn't have missed at this range.* Then he saw it a ribbon of scarlet; blood oozing around the boulder and flowing downhill.

The bad guys started to retreat back up the hill, at least the live ones did. Out of eight vehicles only three made it back up to the crest. Rourke looked around and saw Wes Sanderson's medics and those belonging to the Posse jumping into action with the wounded. *I have got to ask Michael for more information about this Posse of his.*

"ROURKE, JOHN THOMAS ROURKE. Are you still alive?"

"Rourke could see a man with a bullhorn on the crest. Rourke stood up and waved to signal that he was still in the fight. "My name is Frantz Freed. Rourke, you crippled my brother and killed my friend's brother."

Rourke stood up and shouted, "What do you want?"

"We want you, you and your son. There is no need for further bloodshed. Surrender and we'll let your people go. You are the only ones we want." John looked at Michael, then out of the corner of his eye he saw movement.

Akiro Kuriname was approaching, he stopped and bowed. "Greetings Mr. Freed, and my salutations to Mr. Burkholter. You are correct there is no need for further bloodshed. Let us settle this as gentlemen. I will be the champion of my people, send the champion of your people down to fight me in individual combat."

Freed looked at Burkholter. Burkholter nodded. "Do it, but Rourke has to come up also. No, wait... tell him both Rourkes have to come up as sign of good faith"

Putting the bullhorn back close to his mouth Freed said, "We will meet half way down this hillock. Mr. Burkholter and I will be joined by our champion. You Rourkes, both of you, come up here with your man and we will settle this once and for all."

"No, you can't do that. It is a trap," Burger said.

John nodded. "I know it is but one we can use. Who are the best shots on our side?"

Fleming interjected, "Not bragging but I would say Mr. Lynn, Mr. Spivey, Mr. Burger, Mr. Judy and myself."

Rourke turned. "How far do you guess halfway up that hill is?"

Haryett, Fleming's IT man, said, "Six hundred fifty-feet."

Rourke turned back to Fleming. "Who are your best shots at that distance? Who can hit a grapefruit at that distance with one shot and no practice rounds?"

"Spivey, Judy, Burger and me."

Rourke thought a moment. "Okay, I want you and Burger to set up here with your automatics. Spivey, Lynn and Judy as far forward as they can get; you take out Burkholter and Freed. I want the rest of you on personnel. Screw

87

the vehicles; they belong to Spivey, Lynn and Judy." He turned to face Spivey, Lynn and Judy. "Do the three of you have plenty of ammo?" Everyone nodded.

"Michael, do you still have your Kevlar on?"

"Yeah, but you don't." He threw a vest to his father.

"Time's up." The bullhorn sounded. "By the way no weapons, understood?"

Rourke shouted, "I understand! Give us a minute to help the wounded and we'll be up there!" Rourke nodded for Michael to follow him behind cover. "Michael, are both your revolvers loaded?" Michael nodded.

"Leave the rifle, hide the second .44 under your shirt, it will be your back up." Rourke took off his shirt and slipped the double Alessi holster with the twin Detonics on. He shrugged slightly to settle the rig and put his now tattered shirt on without buttoning it.

"Well, hurry it up," the bullhorn sounded again.

"Coming."

"Dr. Rourke," Michael Spivey said, walking forward, "seems you have a slight limp, do you need a cane?" Rourke turned to see Spivey holding what looked like a standard straight walking stick. Spivey gave a slight jerk and Rourke could see there was a blade hidden in it.

Rourke grinned and said, "Yeah, twisted it in the fight. I'll get it back to you."

Spivey smiled. "Good, just a loaner, one of my favorites you know."

"I can see why, not too many two-handed Wakizashis around. Thanks."

Michael had the .44 in the center of his back, next to the copy of Jack Crain's LSX. "How do we play this, Dad?"

John shrugged and started forward. "Don't know, Michael, haven't got a clue, flying by the seat of my pants on this on. Stay alert and be ready and Carpe minutam."

Michael smiled. "Stay alert and ready and seize the minute?"

John replied, smiling, "Yeah, and once you seized the minute, beat your enemy to death with it. We don't have much ammo."

Chapter Forty-One

It was hot and the climb was steep as John and Michael Rourke moved up the hill toward where Akiro Kuriname stood separated by twelve feet from Burkholter and Freed. Burkholter was quiet and intense as he watched the Rourkes approach. Freed's bluster seemed to evaporate the closer the Rourkes came.

A tall, massively built, bald man came down from the hill top to stand next to Freed; he was their champion and John Rourke could see why. With one hand the man ripped the shirt from his chest and flexed. *Impressive,* Rourke thought.

Akiro moved down the hill toward the Rourkes. John had figured the strategy. While taking the high ground was usually the best strategy for defense... it was very easy to lose your balance and improperly calculate speed when on foot and running downhill. Akiro Kuriname had decided to allow gravity to join with the forces of good versus evil.

With Michael on his left and Akiro on his right, John took a pace forward and shouted, "So, you guys are related to Pocked Mark and Woody the Woodpecker, huh? Yeah, I can see the family resemblance now. You two are as ugly and stupid looking as your brothers."

Burkholter bellowed and pulled a three foot long machete from behind his back and charged down the hill. The massively built champion stared for a moment before it sunk in, "It is time to fight." He and Freed took off together but at a slower speed.

John spoke loud enough for Michael and Akiro to hear him. "I'll take Burkholter, Michael you take out the big bald guy and Akiro, that leaves you Mr. Freed."

As Rourke figured, Burkholter's head long rush let his feet outrun his traction. Suddenly, he fell forward landing hard on his face and one shoulder, but keeping the machete. Spitting out grass and blood he started back down the hill, walking now.

The two groups were now within twenty feet of each other when John Rourke said, "Now." Akiro moved straight up toward Freed then side stepped with a reverse back kick that caught Freed in the solar plexus. Freed dropped, trying to breathe while throwing up violently.

Michael raised the .44, fired a quick snap shot and dove to the left in a roll. Coming up into a kneeling position he thumbed the hammer back and sent a round at the massive bald warrior. The slug hit him high in the left shoulder and spun him around.

Rourke hit the release on the cane sword and pulled the blade free. Rourke gripped the hardwood saya in his left hand and the blade in his right. Rourke side stepped up and to the right, ducking under a wild swing of the machete. Using the saya like a baton, he impacted first to Burkholter's gut then hard into the ulnar nerve in his elbow. The machete flew from Burkholter's hand. Rourke stepped back.

Michael was amazed; the bald giant had not gone down, even with an exit wound the size of an apple in his upper back. The big man stood swaying and shaking his head trying to clear it. Michael recocked the Super Blackhawk and said, "Don't do it. My next one will be in your face, sit down and do it now!"

The giant eyes cleared and a vile smile came to his lips. He drew himself to full height and charged. Michael's first shot cut a crease along the side of the big man's cheek. The next one slammed into the bridge of his nose stopping him in mid stride and blowing bone and brains out the back of his head in a spray of pink and gray foam. Then he fell backward, the force of a .44 magnum overcoming even gravity.

Freed wiped vomit from his face and pulled a Philippine Kris knife with a nine-inch blade. Akiro could tell the cutting edges of both sides of the wavy bladed knife were razor sharp, but he did not back up. In fact, he smiled and gracefully stepped forward and motioned for Freed as he said, "Come on. Come and get me."

By now Freed was standing and he lunged holding the knife in a rapier grip trying to stab Kuriname. But Kuriname was no longer there, and he just slapped Freed with his open hand as Freed went by. Freed let out a guttural roar and charged. This time Kuriname stood his ground and accepted the charge full on.

All at once, Kuriname dropped to one knee and in the same motion grabbed the wrist of Freed's knife hand and pulled down. Gravity did the rest. Freed started into a roll as Kuriname reversed the direction of the knife hand; Freed's momentum shoved the sharp blade into his belly. Kuriname stood up and with a flick of his wrist, drew the knife to the side and then released Freed's hand.

Freed landed hard and at the moment of impact, his intestines erupted from the sliced stomach wall. Freed tried to rise up but gave up the effort and laid there entwined in his own intestines. He took four breaths then laid forever still.

Burkholter had regained his machete and transferred it to his left hand; his right was still paralyzed from John Rourke's strike. "I'm gonna cut your heart out Rourke. I'm gonna make you pay."

Rourke spit on the ground and said, "Then do it."

Burkholter charged, swinging the machete in an overhead strike. Rourke easily blocked it and sliced his blade down the left side of Burkholter's body as he passed. Burkholter screamed in pain and charged again, this time swinging wildly in a horizontal slash. Rourke simply stepped back avoiding the blade and stuck the point of his Wakizashi in Burkholter's upper thigh, slicing the femoral artery.

"You might want to sit down," Rourke said and winked at Burkholter whose face turned deep red in rage and he charged again. This time Rourke turned into the charge and with a flick of the razor-sharp Wakizashi's blade, amputating the hand holding the machete. Burkholter stopped and held up his damaged wrist. Blood spurted with each beat of his heart; once from the wrist and once from the severed artery in his leg. He swayed back and forth, first in amazement and then in shock and then he fell.

Then Rourke heard the first gunshot and shouted, "Take cover!" But there was no cover, they had no option but go down as flat as they could get and hope that Fleming and his sharpshooters were as good as he said they were.

Chapter Forty-Two

"General Thorne, may I help you?" Rodney Thorne had picked up the phone from a sound sleep by reflex, he was now fully awake.

"Need you to make a pick-up and delivery for me, General."

Thorne looked at the clock on the dresser: 04:15. "I'm assuming General Sullivan, since it is still the middle of the night, this is an off the books mission."

"Roger that, my office in twenty minutes? Can you make that?"

"Give me thirty minutes, Sir. I'm going to take a shower. Have a sneaking hunch I'm going to need it."

Thirty-five minutes later, Sullivan's orderly knocked on his door and opened it. "He's here, Sir."

"Send him in and bring us coffee."

General Thorne walked in, centered on the desk behind which sat the Chief of Staff and saluted. "General Thorne reporting as ordered, Sir."

Sullivan returned the salute. "Sit down Rodney; sorry to get you out of bed like this but I'm trying to avoid a mess."

Thorne waved the apology aside. "As we say in the Air Force, 'Anytime, anywhere, anyhow.' What's the mission, Sir?"

"I need you to go to these coordinates and pick someone up and take him to these coordinates." Sullivan passed over two slips of paper with coordinates on them. "And no one is to know about this, understood?"

"Yes Sir, I recognize these coordinates. That's where the Alien base is located."

"Correct."

"I am assuming these..." he held up the other coordinates, "are where Dr. Rourke and the President are. Do I take both of them to the Aliens?"

"Correct, you will be picking up several people. And no, I want the President back here first; then you'll take your remaining passengers to that last location. Understood?"

Thorne frowned, saying, "Not really but with your orders, Sir, I'll figure them out while I'm engaged in doing whatever you ordered me to do." The orderly returned with the coffee, Thorne noticed there was only one cup on the tray. "Well, Sir. Thanks for the coffee offer, but I better get hopping. As a song said one time, 'I've got a long way to go and a short time to get there."

"Good plan General and see the orderly at his desk, he has something for you."

Thorne saluted, about faced and walked out. He stopped at the orderly's desk. You have something for me?"

The orderly handed over a Thermos with hot coffee and a bag of sandwiches and chips with a soft drink inside. "General Sullivan said you would like these."

Thorne smiled. "Tell that ol' son of a ... Tell the General I appreciate it."

Chapter Forty-Three

The Grand Hall measured forty-five by sixty-five feet. It was lined with book shelves from floor to ceiling on three sides. Rolling ladders gave a reader access to the higher shelves. The fourth wall was paneled in dark, almost black, wood and at its center was a large fireplace with a fire already set; on either side of the fireplace stood double oak doors ten feet tall.

Six massive chandeliers were supported on chains that were connected to pulleys and used to lower each chandelier to relight or replace the large candles. Each was a heavy wooden wheel, nine feet in diameter and almost five inches thick. On the top surface were twelve wrought iron candle holders screwed into the rim.

A large plain rectangular table sat in the center of the Grand Hall. Its surface was polished but the wood was ancient and worn. Around the table sat forty-eight heavy wood and leather chairs. At the end of the table nearest the lit fireplace sat a larger forty-ninth chair. In front of each chair, sitting almost extraneous to this dark, heavy and solemn atmosphere was an open laptop computer, its screen illuminated and ready for use.

Forty-nine chairs for the Board of Directors; seven times seven, seven is a most significant number in most religions and many cultures. After all, there are seven days of the week, seven colors of the rainbow, seven notes on a musical scale, seven seas and seven ages of man, seven voyages of Sinbad and seven continents.

For mysticism, numbers have importance; the Ancient Babylonians believed the most meaningful number was sixty. Their math and calendar revolved around it. Centuries later, the hour has sixty minutes and the minute sixty seconds. Egypt held twelve as special: twelve realms of the dead, twelve crops, twelve inches to a foot and twelve apostles. A day is split into two cycles of twelve hours and later twelve pennies to a shilling. Twelve and sixty divide neatly into halves, quarters and thirds, making them ideal units of currency and measurement.

But seven, a prime number that cannot neatly be divided by anything other than itself and number one is the most powerful. It honors the mysticism of numerology and prevents a tie vote.

Seven times seven had been the number on this most unique Board of Directors for a long, long time.

Chapter Forty-Four

A soft, barely audible gong sounded and the double oak doors on either side of the lighted fireplace opened. An older, but very attractive woman entered from the left door and began walking forward. Behind her came others.

Another line of walkers began from the left door, but the first person was even with the person directly behind the attractive older woman. In slow, measured step the two lines moved down opposite sides of the long table. She stood at the end of the table while the others stood in front of their assigned places.

A second, barely audible gong sounded and a tall, slender man entered from the right door. He was older than the woman by several years but it was obvious they were brother and sister; it was equally obvious they were a couple. His aquiline nose with prominent bridge sat directly beneath a pronounced Widow's Peak. Where her long, flowing locks were platinum grey with a few crucial dark strands on one side, his raven black hair was cut to a medium length. Grey touched sideburns touched the bottom of his ears.

Both were over six feet tall, the man taller by an inch. They were both perfect physical specimens, but that is where the similarities stopped. They appeared as a dichotomy, divided in appearance into two mutually exclusive, opposed, or contradictory groups. He wore a black suit with black shirt and tie; she wore a white A-line business dress that was form fitting to accentuate the swell of her breasts and hips.

He moved with deliberateness and purpose; she almost floated... an ethereal muse. His jaw was set, his gaze was also; her lips turned up slightly, almost in a smile but not quite. Both had obvious strength. He stood as if an oak tree welcoming the storm's approach; she moved as if a breeze that had the potential of becoming a storm and ripping the forest apart. His stance was one of action; hers... one of thought.

"Welcome, brothers and sisters," his deep voice filling the Grand Hall. "Please, be seated." For a moment the hall was filled with the sound of sliding chairs and movement, but not a word was spoken. "I have asked my sister, Andrea, to begin this meeting with her report. Andrea?"

She stood in place and glancing around made eye contact with each of the other participants. "The time is approaching," she said in voice of perfect pitch and modulation. "Our efforts are about to be rewarded." She smiled, her teeth straight and white. "All of our plans have been set in place by our... associate. Mr. Vale's organization has been most helpful in preparing the way for our ultimate victory.

"Our Russian associates have been equally helpful; however, their attention to detail is not as skillful as Mr. Vale's. Their involvement with the KI has become apparent and that creates concern."

A voice halfway down the table on the left asked, "What about the Alien involvement?"

For an instant her eyes flashed at the interruption; only an instant, however. "I do not consider the Alien issue worth discussing. After all, how much influence can one individual have in the course of our events? Roderick, do you not agree, brother?"

Roderick sat slumped to one side, his elbow braced on the chair arm and his fist supported his chin. He cleared his throat. "Yes, Andrea, one individual, no matter how advanced cannot reasonably have very much influence on the outcome of our plan."

She smiled and gave a slight nod of her head and continued, "Our minions in Michael Rourke's administration as well as our operatives in the Progressive Party are staged to move quickly and forcibly upon our signal. The change of administrations and effective shift of power will take less time than hunting down the Rourke family members and killing each of them.

"Once the purge begins," she smiled... "Once the purge begins, nothing can stop it. The assassination of the indicated 137 individuals and the installation of their replacements will effectively change the government of America for the next 200 years. The Joint Chiefs of Staff, the heads of the FBI, Secret Service, NSA and other intelligence agencies, the Supreme Court and the governors of states not already under control of the Progressive Party will be replaced within seventy-two hours of our plan's initiation."

Another voice said, "That is America... what about the other countries?"

Roderick's hand slammed down on the table, the sound startled many in the room. "I believe that if you will allow Andrea to finish... she will answer your questions before you ask them."

Demurely, Andrea raised her eyes to her brother and smiled again. "Thank you Roderick. The government of the German Republic is now under our control as is the government of New Germany. The assassinations of Manfred Mann and his administration were more complete than we could have asked for. Elections in Spain, England, Lydveldid Island and Australia will begin within the month. All projections show that with actual voting and some manipulations, our candidates will either win outright or we will simply steal the elections.

"China remains a non-player and the central and South American countries have no organic resources that can present problems for us. Mid-Wake will follow the orders of the new American government, so they are not a threat. That leaves the Gallia, or the Wild Tribes of Europe and a few tribal units residing on the African Continent and several others in North and Central America that are remnants of original indigenous nations. We shall simply exterminate these once power has been consolidated and our propaganda program gains momentum."

"That concludes my briefing, Roderick." She sat down.

Roderick stirred and cleared his throat. "Thank you, Andrea. Are there any questions?"

One person, a third of the way down the table on the right, raised his hand and looked at Roderick. Once Roderick acknowledged him with a slight nod, the man stood and said, "What about John Thomas Rourke, Andrea? I find his exclusion from your report... interesting."

Andrea stood. "There is a bit of... confusion concerning Mr. Rourke. As you know he has been missing for some time. We have learned that a rescue mission to a long forgotten Russian underwater base failed to locate him. Ergo, we must assume the following: First, during the mission to Mount Rushmore, John Rourke was either killed, went missing or was captured by person or persons unknown to us at this time. Second, since no explanations have reached the media and the administration has made no mention of it, his death or capture was at the hands of agents we don't know.

"Third, since the attack on New Germany, the death of his son, and the attack we launched on his wife and ex-wife have not caused Rourke to resurface, we must assume that he cannot... therefore we must assume he is dead, disabled or locked away somewhere permanently."

The man shook his head and started to sit. Andrea said, "Do you find my report troubling or inaccurate?"

He stood back up. "Neither Andrea, your report is, as always correct and accurate. I question your conclusion. Do not forget the old adage that when you assume, you make an ass out of you and me." He sat down then said, "I have studied John Rourke, you can assume nothing, nothing where he is concerned. Until I see his head myself, I consider him to still be a threat." The room sat hushed, no one in the room had a memory of the last time someone had spoken to Andrea that way...and survived.

Chapter Forty-Five

The Captain sat meditating alone in his cabin. *I have lost count of the number of days and weeks and years we have traveled, but soon it will be over. Soon, we will have regained control of that which is rightfully ours.*

A trill sounded and the Captain stood and turned to face the door to his quarters. "Enter."

"Zdravstvujtye, Captain," the Russian Spetsnaz Colonel said using the formal greeting.

The Captain was not in the mood for the normal linguistics sparring. "What do you want, Colonel?"

The Colonel's smile disappeared as he sat down. "Is something wrong?"

"Yes, Colonel, many things are wrong. First of all, I have issues with your manners. You are not allowed to sit in my presence unless you are invited to do so."

The Colonel slowly stood and assumed the position of attention. "My apologies, Captain. I did not mean to be disrespectful."

"Second, I want to know what you have found out about the loss of our aircraft."

"As I have said, Captain, I know of nothing in the land, sea or air based arsenals of any government on the surface capable of destroying those craft. Further, there is no evidence of a catastrophic malfunction of one or both of the craft. While, as I said, some incredible pilot error…"

"My people don't make errors, Colonel."

Colonel Mikhail Sergeyevich smiled. "Then, as I said before we have another player in the game."

"Where is your proof? And do not refer to you Occam's razor problem-solving game."

"But Captain…"

"Yes, I know. The simplest answer is usually the correct answer."

"Exactly," The Colonel's manner softened. "Tell me my friend, do you feel well? You seem unusually tense."

The Captain's face hardened, he would not tell this fool he had not been sleeping or that when he slept his dreams were scrambled and fearful. Full of times so long ago, he had almost forgotten them. Full of things he had done, so long ago. Full of a betrayal so despicable there was no redemption possible.

"Colonel Sergeyevich, I tire of these delays. It is time to act. And if you are correct that the Alien race my people dealt with so long ago has returned, it is time to destroy them as well."

Sergeyevich smiled. "I could not agree more, Captain. I shall order the final preparations, with your permission of course."

"Permission granted, now leave me." Sergeyevich gave a nod and turned to leave. "Are you certain the Aliens are here, Colonel?"

Sergeyevich sensed anxiety in the Captain's voice. He turned and said simply, "I am certain of nothing other than our great victory, Captain."

Chapter Forty-Six

The Egg settled on the helicopter pad next to the White House, the hatch opened and Michael Rourke took off at a jog toward the presidential residence. It was 0100 hours local and the White House area lights were shut off. John Thomas Rourke turned to face General Rodney Thorne. "Let's go, Rodney."

"Roger that, Sir." Thorne handed Rourke a note. "Welcome back, Sir. These are the coordinates we are going to be landing at and the order we have to get to each location. These will be to pick up packages, a few minutes at each location. The last one you already know where that will be and we will be staying there quite a while." Thorne plugged in the coordinates, checked the flight plans.

"Let's go."

*****

The Egg flew into the opening of the tunnel; it was almost forty feet across and half that distance tall. Thorne maintained his focus and expertly guided the craft to a soft landing in a circular area easily 300 feet in diameter. Directly in front of The Egg were three doors approximately twenty feet wide and that tall. Rourke stepped out of The Egg and walked toward the center one and stood there for a moment.

After several more minutes, he raised his hand to bang on the door. Before his hand could make contact on the first strike... the door whished open.

There The Creator stood. Elongated body and a small chest... legs shorter than what one would expect in a human, the humeri and the thighs appeared to be the same length as the forearms and shins... no visible sexual characteristics... Head, unusually large in proportion to the body... no hair visible anywhere on the body, including the face... no noticeable outer ears or nose, only small openings or orifices for ears and nostrils... mouth small... opaque black eyes, very large but with no discernible iris or pupil... about four feet tall, maybe slightly more but only by an inch or two...

In its right hand was the silver headband. The creature held it up and Rourke nodded, stepped forward and took the headband and placed it on his head.

I... felt... your... presence... your... coming... back. I... did... not... think... to... see... you... again. The words of The Creator once again sounded in Rourke's mind.

"I am sorry for that; I assumed you knew I would be back. Something has happened, or is happening. I wanted to both warn you and ask for your help."

Warn... is... there... danger? Is... it... the... Others?

Rourke nodded.

What... help... can... I... provide?

"Tell me who started the war."

Long... ago... we... came... here... in... peace. We... were... looking... for... what... we... call... ἀμβροσία.

"ἀμβροσία? I believe ἀμβροσία is what my people call chlorophyll, correct?"

Correct. It... is... necessary... for... life... to... my... people. We... found... it... in... abundance... on... your... world. There... is... more... ἀμβροσία... here... than... in... any... place... in... the... known... six... galaxies. We... thought... we... had... found... a... way... to... save... our... dying... people... instead... our... people... were... destroyed... by... the... Others.

"Tell me what happened."

You... do... not... know? How... is... that... possible?

Rourke frowned. "The story was lost to time. The Others, as you call them, were merely a legend, a story to us. We did not know if they ever truly existed."

And... my... people?

"You were less than a legend, less than a story; your people were a distant fear. Something that was not known to be real but still filled my people with fear. You were like noises in the night we could not explain so our imagination filled in the gaps with monsters."

Chapter Forty-Seven

She had pushed against General Sullivan's resistance until he had finally given in; a little. He would authorize a quick trip to Göbekli Tepe, a very quick trip. She had 48 hours to locate and, if possible, retrieve whatever information she felt was there. Natalia now stood facing the graves; all that remained of the campsite she had almost been raped in. Her clock was ticking.

Nearby, the ancient structures known as Göbekli Tepe sat on a flat and barren plateau. Now building ruins fanned in all directions. In the months since her disastrous mission to Göbekli Tepe, work had continued. Excavations on the southern slope had found the remains of tools.

More ruins were now evident and the size of the complex was far larger than it had been the last time she walked this ground. Walls, compounds, even a square building foundation had been located. It might have been the remains of a Roman watchtower, but no one knew for sure.

The exposed complex measured over twenty acres in size.

Neolithic quarrying had produced blocks that had been used in the construction of the temple complex. Several T-shaped pillars that had not been levered out of the bedrock were uncovered. The largest lay on the northern plateau; it was over twenty feet long with a head over ten feet across and weighed probably fifty tons.

It was one of these T-shaped pillars she had come to inspect. It had been discovered amongst flint and limestone fragments that suggested a workshop dedicated to sculptures. When found, it had been laid down; "carefully laid down" was the description from the head archaeologist. "Had it fallen, it would have shattered. There were also remnants of rope that probably were used to lower it safely to the ground." Like the other T-shaped pillars, it had carvings on it.

But it was when the pillar had been raised and secured that the buzz of activity stopped and a radio call went out to both Mid-Wake and the White House. There were carvings on this pillar. One in particular was most reminiscent of the overturned figure eight that stood for "Infinity," but incorporating something eerily reminiscent of the mathematical symbol for "pi" and a sword behind it.

The other resembled several unusual gold ornaments that were thought to be pre-Columbian, from around 500-800 CE. These had been discovered in Colombia, Costa Rica, Peru and Venezuela. They appeared to have delta shaped main wings and a set of smaller wings near the tail; the body was wide and marked by designs and a tall "tail fin" was mounted on the rear. When they were first found, it was thought they were zoomorphic—representing animals. However, there was also speculation they were something else; some Archaeologists interpreted them as model airplanes.

Natalia had recognized both immediately. The first, the overturned figure eight with the mathematical symbol for "pi" and a sword behind it, had been on a uniform buckle John Rourke had taken off a dead Alien who had crashed his UFO in Canada before the Night of the War. The second was not a zoomorphic representation of some animal nor was it a model for an airplane. It was a representation of one of the ships of the KI.

The last carving on this T-shaped pillar showed what appeared to be a great battle between ships of the KI and egg shaped objects that reminded Natalia of the UFO that General Rodney Thorne now flew.

She turned to her companion. He wore a robe, saffron in color and his hair and beard were long and snow white. "Have you ever seen anything like this?"

He studied the carving intensely, walked close to the pillar and laid his hands on the stone. Softly, gently... as though he was caressing the lines of the carving, he closed his eyes. Tears leaked out his closed lids and rolled down his cheeks to be lost in his beard. When he opened his eyes, he was pale.

"Your archaeologist was correct. This pillar had been laid down on purpose," The Keeper said solemnly. "This is the depiction of the end of my world. I am guessing that one of my people survived the destruction and gave the story to your ancestors who kept the memory alive as a verbal legend. Evidently it was known to someone that carved it on this pillar. But that would have been possibly 30,000 years after the event."

"But my people did not know this story until you came."

The Keeper nodded. "This could well be the one and only time the story was ever 'written down' or recorded, and the pillar was laid down to protect the carvings. Probably very few of your people ever saw this carving; maybe only the carver. Then this entire complex was not just abandoned... remember it was purposely covered by the very people that worshiped here and no one could figure out why. This... this carving could be the reason."

"But why here?"

"Twelve thousand years ago, this area was probably a paradise. It sat at the northern edge of what your people called the Fertile Crescent. It had a mild climate and arable land and would have attracted hunter-gatherers from incredible distances. Your own archaeologist found no evidence that people permanently lived here. I suspect, as they do, it was a place of worship on an unprecedented scale; it could have been mankind's first 'cathedral on a hill.' Where else would you put your most important stories to protect them?"

She set up the 3D laser scanning device that could reveal tool marks made centuries ago on the face of this slab. Even those that now would be invisible to the naked eye. These would show up in unprecedented precision and hopefully show the actual true history of the battle between the KI and the Aliens so long ago. At least that was the plan.

As she turned, she hesitated... something gnawed at her consciousness, or at least at her awareness. She looked around, but there was nothing that appeared to be out of place, out of the normal. Then she saw him.

Chapter Forty-Eight

We... were... not... the... monsters. The... Others... were... the... monsters. We... had... been... here... for... many... of... your... years... obtaining... and... processing... the... ἀμβροσία. When... we... arrived... there... were... no... beings... on... this... world... like... you... or... the... Others. We... watched... you... develop... we... watched... you... crawl... out... of... the... ooze... and... crawl... on... all... fours... and... then... stand... and... walk... up... right. We... felt... a... bond... with... those... creatures. Ages... ago... on... our... own... world... similar... things... had... happened... and... they... were... the... birth... of... my... people.

"You are saying your people evolved?"

We... assume... so... but... there... are... no... records... of... those... times. Some... believe... we... changed... over... time... moving... from... one... appearance... to... finally... the... one... you... see... before... you. Others... believe... this... is... the... way... we... have... always... looked... but... our... minds... grew... as... we... learned.

Rourke smiled. "My people struggle with the same questions. Another way we are alike, your people and mine."

Our... bodies... are... different... Your... people... communicate... verbally... mine... do... not. The... device... allows... you... to... hear... my... thoughts... it... does... not... allow... me... to... hear... yours. What... is... the... warning... you... bring?

"The Others, I believe they prepare for war against both of our peoples."

They... align... with... some... of... you... against... the... rest... of... you... and... me?

"Yes."

Chapter Forty-Nine

He was standing near some of the native workers, ones that had moved dirt from one of the channels the archaeologists had directed them to dig. He appeared benign, simply another worker from a village somewhere across the windblown plains that circled Göbekli Tepe.

He looks familiar, she thought, then shrugged. *Maybe not, it is probably just this place, this place of death and my almost rape.* Then the man turned and looked directly in her eyes before turning quickly and moving away from the other workers.

Natalia spun and ran after him. Her right had reached behind her and pulled the Bali-Song knife from her right rear pocket. Across the plains came a new sound... click, click, click... click, click, click... click, click and she caught up to him.

Grabbing his tunic, she pivoted to the side and fell forward, pulling him over and backward. She rolled quickly to the left and in an instant sat straddling the man's chest, with fire in her eyes and the Bali-Song weaving and shining circles in the air above the man's eyes. Click, click, click... click, click, click... click, click, click!

The blade locked open and jumped toward the man's throat; stopping just as a thin line of blood formed across the man's voice box. "Tell me," she whispered coming closer to the man's face. "Tell me who you are and why you are here."

The man glared at her but said nothing. The blade of the Bali-Song slid to the right, just a bit. More blood and Natalia smiled into the man's eyes; "You may tell me... you may not. You may live to see the end of this day or only the end of your life." Natalia Tiemerovna-Rourke, former Major in the Russian KGB had returned.

The man smiled and spoke... in perfect Russian, this "Turkish" worker spoke in perfect Russian. "Bitch, you traitorous bitch; I may die but so will you and your family and your children. But certainly that bastard John Thomas

Rourke shall die and the democracy your kind of filth protects and serves. He was right about you."

"Who?" she shouted. "Who was right about me? Tell me now and I promise you a quick death. Do it or I will flay you alive and feed your eyes to the crows."

The man looked at her and started to speak, all he got out was "Karamat..." before she sliced across his voice box and into the carotid artery on the right side of his neck. With a quick reverse of the blade the carotid on the left side was severed. She had lied, she never intended to give him a quick death... but she never thought he would say the name of that bloodthirsty evil bastard from so long ago; her long dead husband, Colonel Vladimir Karamatsov. He had tortured her, raped her and Rourke had tried to kill him but he had survived. Natalia had finally killed him herself.

The dying man did not struggle; he simply laid there with an evil smile on his face as his life's blood pumped out onto the dry gravelly ground.

When the blood no longer pumped, she felt a hand on her shoulder; a gentle hand. Looking up she saw The Keeper with a look of abject sorrow on his face; he moved the hand from her shoulder and held it out for her to grasp and stand up. Softly he said, "Come, my dear. It is time for us to leave."

Natalia wiped the blade on the man's tunic and slowly stood up. With a click, click, click... the blade was locked in its handle and the Bali-Song disappeared back into her pocket. "I recognized him," she said as her breathing slowed. "It has been so very long I almost did not. His disguise is very good, but he could not hide his eyes. Not from me. He is from my ex-husband's cadre of followers."

The Keeper nodded and after a moment asked, "Then it is true?"

Natalia nodded. "I am sorry to say it is. Once, when Vladimir was 'punishing me' for an imagined lapse of decorum, this pig watched as he beat me. Watched and laughed... I often dreamed of killing him, I prayed one day to kill him but thought him dead before my world ended."

"What does it all mean?"

She drew a deep breath, "There is an old saying, 'When the gods want to punish you, they answer your prayers. My prayer has finally been answered, but now I know truly how much danger my family… and the world… really, truly are in."

Chapter Fifty

Two rescue VTOLs had picked up the survivors of the crash of Air Force One and the subsequent battle with the Neo-Nazis. One took the POTUS Posse and Chief Warrant Officer Wes Anderson's men and Akiro's Dog Soldiers back to Fantastic Caverns, the new Rourke Retreat, to finish preparations. The other secured the scene and waited on additional aircraft that would be able to salvage Air Force One herself.

Two days later, Sanderson's men and the Dog Soldiers' conditions bordered on exhaustion, but not only was the work schedule moving forward at an acceptable rate, but morale was pretty good. Sanderson and Kuriname were in the main tent going through the construction schedule and layout of the new Retreat.

Sanderson laid out a blow up from an old brochure. "You can see what the Fantastic Caverns looked like before The Night of the War. Near the Hall of Giants is where John Knox and his dog originally found the entrance to the cavern in 1862. Near the Breakdown Room is the second and larger entrance."

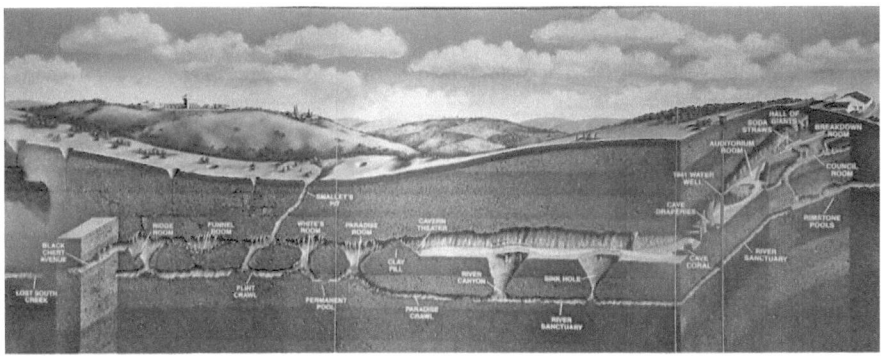

"As a crow flies, what is left of the old Springfield Airport lies just about three miles away to the southwest. This vertical structure on the left side is the old control tower."

Kuriname pointed out, "Damn shame the terrain is so torn up, would make for easier transport if it looked more like it used too."

Sanderson nodded. "Now, between the Cavern Theater and the Cave Coral is where the residential area will be located. It is furthest from the cavern entrances and provides the greatest protection. The Auditorium Room will be the Communication Center and Operational Headquarters. Adjacent to the 1941 water well piping is a system of antennae that can be raised and lowered as required. These are both passive receptors as well as dynamic transmitters.

"The Breakdown Room will function as the primary storage area for fuel and water as well as the primary garage for all vehicles. On the far side of the hill top, the third entrance to the cavern system has been discovered and will function as a hanger and work area for The Egg and several small aircraft. Underground access between the two cavern systems keeps everything from prying eyes.

"A secondary personnel emergency exit has been created to exit at Smalley's Pit. Modifications beginning at the cavern theater through the Paradise Crawl and White's Room include expanding of the passageway, separate lighting systems and flooring to allow for speedy egress when needed. Additional counter-illumination generators have been set up and camouflaged near the exit.

"Another emergency exit will follow the lower system from the Paradise Room that is marked River Sanctuary to the Rimstone Pools at Indian Spring and finally empties into the Little Sac River. This is however, only going to be available during the dry season. The rest of the year it is flooded or nearly so with drain water from the area."

"So," Akiro asked, "when will it be habitable?"

"It's habitable now, if we had to inhabit it. The more time we have the more refined it can become. Glad your guys are here. That'll really help."

Akiro Kuriname stood alone on the ledge above the Fantastic Cavern's main entrance, watching the activity below. To the uninitiated eye there was not much to see, but that was a false narrative.

Counter-illuminating camouflage generators protected an area that was now the size of several football fields and still expanding. The movement of water storage tanks, fuel storage tanks and the like had cut deep ruts in the grass covered soil. *We'll have to fix that,* he made a note. *Should the generators ever fail, that will stand out like an arrow pointing to us.*

An alarm sounded on his head set. "Kuriname, go ahead, over."

"Sir, we have just made contact with Mr. Rubenstein. He's about thirty minutes out, over."

Kuriname smiled and checking his watch added, "Excellent, just about on schedule. Are they alright and is the equipment alright? Over."

"Haskins... Haskins didn't make it, Sir. They ran into problems crossing the Mississippi, over."

Kuriname cursed under his breath. "Is Rubenstein okay? What about the cargo, any damages? Over."

"Yes Sir, Mr. Rubenstein and the cargo are fine. He is bringing Haskins' body back, Sir. Over."

*****

Paul Rubenstein passed the counter-illuminating generators on the west side of the caverns, pulled to a stop in front of Kuriname, shut off the truck and stepped down stiffly from the cab.

"Good to see you, Paul."

"Good to see you, Akiro, didn't think I would get the opportunity again."

Akiro looked at Paul then waved four men over to the truck. "Haskins?"

"The trailer, you'll have to move the Harley." The four men moved quickly to retrieve the body while a team of others began moving cargo to pre-designated areas within the main cavern.

"Status report?" Paul asked.

Kuriname cleared his throat and began, "We found John, he is alive."

"Thank God, is he alright?"

Kuriname nodded. "Yes, good physically, somewhat in overwhelm after finding out what all had transpired since he went missing. He will remain incognito while he is checked out medically and the 'relocation' is being initiated."

Paul nodded. "The family..."

Akiro said, smiling, "Annie is with Natalia, Sarah and Emma at a safe house. Emma's father and brother are along in charge of the security detail guarding them. Otto Croenberg will be joining them as soon as he gets back from Europe. The children are in protective custody at a location away from Camp Zero."

Paul nodded and looked around then back at Kuriname. "I want to make contact with Annie as soon as possible."

Kuriname nodded, "We'll have a secure line for you in just a few minutes."

Paul nodded. "Thanks." Looking around again he said, "You and your men have been busy here. A lot has been done."

"Still more to do," Kuriname said. "We did have one good piece of luck while you were gone. A team was making an exploration of the main caverns and found a side system that opened up on the west side of the Retreat 2."

"Retreat 2... Is that what we're calling it now?"

Kuriname nodded. "Anyway, that side system has a main room that is almost as large of The Hall of Giants. In fact the room is taller; I think we're going to use that area for a garage and hanger. We can't get a full size VTOL in there, but The Egg or a smaller plane should fit.

"A lot was involved with the process that created the Caverns and it began a very long time ago," Kuriname continued. "Part of the cave formation was going on in the Ozarks since seismic activity pushed the rocks up from a shallow sea that once covered the region. While it is difficult to tell the exact age of a cave, we know that Fantastic Caverns is thousands of years old; probably tens of thousands... maybe hundreds of thousand years old.

"The hilly topography and abundant limestone found in the Ozarks make it an ideal setting for cave formation. Just add water and the list of ingredients is complete. As the water percolates through the porous limestone, it chemically eats away at the rock, leaving the voids and cavities that grow into caves, some of which are quite extensive. Some Missouri cave systems were known to be more than twenty miles long.

"I suspect that as we continue to explore the Caverns we are very likely to discover much more about them. I wouldn't be surprised if we find other openings, other caves and other rooms. The Night of the War and the centuries since then may well have made significant changes to the caverns that we will simply have to find.

"We have already found some changes and some artifacts, even some information about the Caverns that survived in a time capsule someone thought to put in the cavern. Prior to The Night of the War, humans never inhabited these Caverns; however, a variety of animals did find a home here.

"The grotto salamander, the cave crayfish and the rare, blind Ozarks cavefish, a reclusive little creature no longer than a finger, still live in the Fantastic Caverns. Clean, unpolluted groundwater is vital to these animals and to the cave's overall health. That's why water quality was carefully monitored. We have recently found artifacts that show that for some period of time after The Night of the War, the Caverns were inhabited by people that had survived the initial bombings. How many lived here and for how long... we may never know."

"Let me check in with Annie and then I want to take a look at it," Paul said. "What is the location of the rescue team? I want to speak with Michael for sure and John if that's possible."

Chapter Fifty-One

One of the Communication Central technicians monitoring the satellite feed motioned for his supervisor. Master Sergeant Lancon walked over and plugged in his head set to the consol. "What do you have, Airman?"

The technician shook his head, saying, "Not sure Sergeant, I have three individuals on horseback approaching the caverns from the east. They are still about four miles away but whether they mean to or not they are headed directly at us."

Lancon keyed his microphone and reported, "Three approaching on horseback about four miles out. Appear to be on a direct course to us." Lancon gave the coordinates where the three would intercept the Caverns' counter-illuminating camouflage field.

Chief Wes Sanderson acknowledged the transmission, scrambled a squad of his marines to that location and beckoned for Paul Rubenstein to join him. They headed back into the Cavern toward Communication Central where Lancon stood with his hand on the technician's shoulder. "Airman First Class Jeter, switch to thermal imaging and sweep that area." Lancon had indicated a deep overgrown gorge. The floor, nearly three hundred feet below the lip of the gorge, was totally obscured from view by the thick canopy of trees.

The scan showed no heat signatures. Lancon magnified the image... still no heat signatures. "Looks like it is just the three of them, Chief. No way to know if they are just out riding or purposely headed for us."

Sanderson growled, "I don't give a damn which it is, if they try to penetrate our parameter, I want them taken and brought directly to me. Alive, if possible but frankly... I don't particularly care. Bottom line is they can't be allowed to leave without us knowing why they came."

Sanderson's radio beeped a soft chirp; he keyed the shoulder mic. Red One, go ahead. This is Red Leader. Over."

A whispered voice came back, "They are just sitting there Red Leader, about fifty yards from the parameter, just sitting on the horses. Over."

Sanderson asked, "Are they armed? Over."

"Yes, Chief, two men and a boy. The men have hunting rifles... don't see any handguns but I can't be sure. The boy seems to only have a longbow... but again, can't be sure. They are wearing long coats, dusters I think is what the old cowboys called them. Over."

"What are they doing? Over."

"Just sitting on their horses, Chief. Wait a minute, they are dismounting. One man seems to be collecting wood and the boy is collecting rocks... why, he is building a fire ring. I think they are making camp. Over."

Sanderson frowned. "What about the other man? Over."

"He is just standing there looking in this direction. Just standing there. Over." A few minutes passed. "Red Leader, this is Red One. They have a fire going and have loosened the cinches on the saddles. Over."

"Red One, have they dropped the saddles yet? Over."

"Negative... no they haven't. They have hobbled the horses and are just letting them graze. Looks like they are making coffee. Over."

Several more minutes passed. "Red Leader, this is Red One. Over."

"Go ahead Red One. Over."

"Red Leader, the guy that has just been standing and staring in our direction..."

"Go ahead Red One, what about him. Over."

"He just walked over to his saddlebag and removed a white flag on a short staff. He is waving it back and forth... Now he has stuck the flag staff in the ground and has walked back to the campfire and is pouring coffee. Over."

Paul looked at Sanderson. "What the hell, Chief?"

Sanderson shrugged his shoulders and smiled. "I surmise the following: Number one, they know we are here. Number two, they want to talk under a flag of truce." Sanderson pulled his side arm and did an unnecessary check to be sure there was a round in the chamber. "And three, it appears coffee's on. Do you want a cup?"

Chapter Fifty-Two

Sanderson passed the binoculars to Rubenstein. The two men they saw were as different as day and night. One was slender and bald; the other was taller, heavier with dark hair and a bushy dark beard. The bald man moved with an economy of fluid motion. The boy appeared to be around twelve or thirteen-years old and stayed close to the bald man. *Probably his son,* Paul decided. The darker man seemed in charge of things but it wasn't the rigid formality of a military relationship.

Sanderson keyed his microphone. "Any others in the area? Over."

Lancon's voice came back, "Negative... at least no one visible or on thermals."

Sanderson turned to Paul. "Your call."

Paul nodded and sat quietly for a long moment. "That coffee smells pretty good, Chief. Let's get a cup."

"Roger that, Sir... but remember the plan." Paul nodded and Sanderson changed to the team frequency and keyed the mic again. "Okay, Troopers. We're going in. Stand by and be ready for anything." Changing the frequency back he radioed to Lancon, "Turn it off, Master Sergeant." Seconds later, the counter-illuminating camouflage field shimmered, faded and disappeared.

The tall, dark man shifted his position and stood up as Chief Sanderson and Rubenstein stood and walked toward him. "Hello, my name is James White. This is my friend Lane Alexander and his son, Noah." As they drew closer, White extended his hand in greeting.

"I'm Marine Chief Warrant Officer Wes Sanderson," Sanderson said, shaking the proffered hand. "This is Dr. William Elliot, he is a geologist. We are conducting studies in this area for the government. May I ask where you are from?"

Alexander and his son poured two cups of coffee and brought them to Sanderson and "Elliot." Alexander fielded the questions. "We're from the Underground. Sir, I'm looking for two of my citizens. They went missing two days ago but had left word they would be in this area." White described the two.

"Well, Mr. White," Sanderson said, "you have located them; one is dead and the other is a prisoner."

White did not appear overly surprised at the news but said, "I don't understand Mr. Sanderson... One dead... the other a prisoner..."

"Chief, Chief Sanderson. That's my rank. Yes Sir, one dead, one prisoner. Your 'citizens' opened fire on my encampment. The boy that died was sniping at my men while his partner, an older man, was apparently spotting targets for him. Those targets were my people. What can you tell me about their actions?"

White held up his hands. "Nothing, Chief Sanderson. This makes no sense, these were two fine citizens. A father and son out on a hunting trip, there must be some mistake..."

Sanderson nodded. "The mistake was made by your people. They shot at us and the boy died and his father was wounded. You said you're from the Underground. You are part of a militia?" Sanderson asked.

White laughed out loud. Alexander smiled; he had a quick and friendly smile. "No, no... The old Springfield Underground. It is a series of storage vaults, a hundred feet underground. Our ancestors took refuge there centuries ago when the war started."

"Dr. Elliot" said, "Really, how is it we've never heard of such a place? We have not seen any evidence of a town."

White said, smiling, "You won't. Fanton is underground. We really haven't had that much contact with the outside world. I suppose we were simply forgotten about when the war started."

Chapter Fifty-Three

"Just after World War II, a family developed the Underground. It began back in 1946, when the father arrived in the area and started mining limestone for agricultural lime to build the nutrients back into the soil after the Dust Bowl days.

"He had worked in road construction and he used his experience to develop both truck and rail transportation systems to ship out the mined limestone. Eventually, the mining resulted in immense underground galleries that could be used for storage. When the war came, there was little warning... but there was enough for many people to evacuate to the Underground. It turned out to be the largest fallout shelter to survive on North America."

"How big is this place?" Sanderson asked.

"About two and a half million square feet, but we are constantly making more space available as our population grows," White said.

Sanderson shifted his position next to the fire. "So... how can we help you, Mr. White?"

White smiled and said, "Well, Chief... I do appreciate the offer but I kinda figured it was us that could help you." White's eyes twinkled and he glanced at Dr. Elliot. "You and Mr. Rubenstein, I'm sorry to blow your cover Mr. Rubenstein but you are, after all, a famous man."

Paul smiled back. "And you Mr. White are a well-read man." He pointed at the tassels that were tied to White's belt loops; Paul recognized them. "Tzitzis?"

White smiled. "Very good, Mr. Rubenstein. Yes, Tzitzis. As you know they are to remind us of standards or rules or laws. God said we should have standards in everything we do; eating, talking, and dressing." White flashed a smile. "Even about sleeping and going to the bathroom. With these standards we bring God into each and every action of our lives.

"But you are not Jewish are you Mr. White?"

"Not Jewish in the context you are speaking of, Mr. Rubenstein. But, I do adhere to certain Jewish concepts. The Laws of Judaism were created long ago for the specific purpose of adding spiritual aspects to our physical natures. Or, another way to say it is that by focusing on physical acts, we in turn are focusing on the spiritual."

"Interesting combination," Paul said.

"Combination?" White raised his eye brows in question.

"The Tzitzis hang from your belt loops and the .45 in your shoulder holster and the knife on your belt; interesting combination."

White sat upright and closed his jacket, buttoning it. "You are observant, Mr. Rubenstein."

"That's how I've stayed alive so long," Paul said, smiling. "Why..." Paul started to ask.

"Why wear them? Two reasons. The Torah says during the days when my people hunted each other, it was the color and construction of the Tzitzis that identified your clan."

Paul nodded. "My understanding is that the color was optional as long as there was one blue string incorporated in each tassel. Perhaps this is something unique to your people."

"We wear them to honor God and to remember those that were murdered during the Dark Times," White responded. "Let me explain. Before the bombs started falling, the population of Springfield, Missouri was less than 150,000. When they stopped falling... there was less than 20,000 huddled in the Underground. When the war came, my ancestors found they had amongst themselves architects, scientists, and doctors. They banded together and became known as 'The Team;' their idea was to save as many as could be saved.

"The Team realized that survival from the initial destruction was a short lived victory. Following the first attack, they reasoned that geological upheavals and fault failures would redraw this continent. Earth itself would become our enemy, it would be dangerous. Climate change, radiation, social breakdown, and God only knew what else... how could you prepare for things that literally were beyond comprehension?"

"Well," Paul said, "it looks like they did a pretty good job of it."

"Yes, but it was not without its cost. It took over 250 years before this region had an inhabitable surface. During that time, many generations were born underground. Survival became our greatest concern with birth control strenuously enforced. Population management was not the only concern; unfortunately our citizens did not always behave correctly. It was a very dark time with many tremendous and diabolical mistakes made. We refer to those times as 'The Lost Ages.'

"The Team really only made two mistakes. The first was how long we would be underground. After a while, the Scientific Corps learned to map and manipulate our genes. That eliminated most of the consequences of inbreeding within such a small population. Our engineered citizens were quite... improved, would be a good word."

Paul frowned, genetic manipulations... "Eugenics," Paul said, "I am familiar with it. The word comes from the Greek words for 'well-born' and 'race.' It is a set of beliefs and practices that aims at improving the genetic quality of the human race."

"Yes, it was a social philosophy that advocated the improvement of human traits through selective breeding of people with more desired traits or positive Eugenics," White said. "People with less-desired or undesired traits or negative Eugenics were restricted from breeding and were even sterilized."

Paul nodded. "Many governments before The Night of the War either purposefully practiced Eugenics or minimally quietly proposed it. The worse example, Nazi Germany, but do not forget Sweden, England... even the United States had advocates promoting selective breeding."

"We simply perfected it," White said. "Today, we live longer than the 'Naturals' and we are stronger and smarter... we are truly a well born race. The Team had made excellent provisions for The Awakening, we returned to the surface. Within the underground facility, we could monitor conditions on the surface. When it was time, we pretty well knew what to expect. There was a time capsule The Team had created for the Awakening. It contained instructions on how to save whatever was left of humanity; if there were any."

Chapter Fifty-Four

There... is... no... purpose... in... conflict. It... is... destructive.

"Agreed. Tell me more about the Others," Rourke said.

They... developed... more rapidly... than... the... rest... of... the... creatures... like... yourself. While... those... like... you... communicated... with... grunts... and... growls... the... Others... were... building... settlements. Their... knowledge... grew... at... an... incredible... rate. We... watched... but... did... not... allow... contact... between... our... peoples... any... longer. Contact... was... forbidden. They... grew... taller... than... others... of... your... species... and... smarter.

"But contact was eventually made again?"

Yes... by... accident. A... group... of... them... stumbled... on... one... of... our... processing... operations. One... of... what... you... call... our... counter-illuminating... generators... had... malfunctioned. They... saw... us... they... saw... our... process. Once... contact... had... been... made... it... could... not... be... unmade.

"They had no idea where your facilities were before that?"

No... it... had... been... many... generations... with... no... contact. They... had... forgotten... we... were... here.

Chapter Fifty-Five

"You said The Team made two mistakes; what was the other?" Paul asked.

"Social Fracture..." White said.

"What do you mean?"

"There was a segment that... for whatever reason, chose not to return to the surface. They understood living underground. It was easy; the machinery the Team had created maintained our life support system. There were generations of practice, research and development. Plus, I believe those people wrapped themselves in a blanket of superiority. They began referring to themselves as the Complexians and those that lived on the surface as The Toppers.

"It was hard work living on the surface. Had it not been for the library, everyone would have starved. But again, The Team had provided very well for the future. We had seeds for vegetables, fruit, yes... even flowers. There were heritage seeds, nothing genetically engineered, once planted the resulting plants were fertile. They created more seeds from each of their species.

"We had tools and the survivors were operating as planned; utilizing the tools, machinery and knowledge of the late 19th and early 20th centuries. For a while, everything was as the Team had expected. It was a great cooperative effort in which both sides supported the efforts of the other."

"You said... for a while."

"About twenty years, then it began to change... everything changed. One day it all ended."

"What happened?" Paul asked.

"A new leader arose and suddenly it was realized that government and religion were no longer separate. The problem was we had two governments and two religions that sprang into being almost overnight."

Paul shook his head. "But your people had been working together, side by side for generations."

White nodded. "True, but that all changed into a big hoax, the biggest of all time. The original teachings from The Team were now reinterpreted. Suddenly people began to disappear and the two groups began waiting on the arrival of the 'Messiah.'

"Christians went into in a panic. Complexians went into a religious fervor. Toppers went crazy. Hoaxes abounded, especially 'found' documents and 'relics'; all were false but many people were caught off-guard. Often times Scripture was misunderstood or purposely misinterpreted. Many learned too late that the doctrines they've put all their faith into were not just wrong... but manipulated fakes.

"Those leading the two groups developed immense egos. No longer were they seeking the truth from the Lord Himself. They did not want to be told they were wrong... about anything. No one wanted to hear that such a possibility even existed. A false sense of calm developed only to be replaced by terror and death.

"We had been cast out of our world by World War III. That world became a wasteland and we sought shelter underground. When the opportunity came for us to reclaim the surface, we soon realized that the life we had known and enjoyed was over. Then my ancestors managed to corrupt the new world. Corrupt it as their ancestors had. For a while it seemed as though we had escaped God's wrath and judgment.

"But that was not to be, even to those who were of the same bloodlines, the 'same seed and heritage.' There came a time when we hunted each other like animals. Worse than the Lost Ages; those years are known as the Dark Times. We found places where someone had stocked supplies for the End of the World and the end of the world came... but they died before they could use them. In some cases, people had no idea how to prepare something for long time storage and supplies were useless.

"Once we found a shipping container that had been converted into a bunker and buried. There were boxes and boxes of food and ammunition neatly stacked on dozens of shelves from ceiling to floor. Unfortunately they were still in their original boxes... and only in their boxes, not in ammo cans. No protective covering for the food. Probably in less than two years after The Night of the War, all of it... literally thousands of rounds was totally useless. In other collapsed buildings, we've found guns in the same shape, stuck in a closet, under beds or buried in the ground... none of them stored correctly, totally useless.

"Occasionally, we would find a treasure... properly stored, hermetically sealed... perfect condition. Luckily for us, there were a lot of folks that were ready. We have guns that are centuries old and just as functional as the day they were made."

"What about parts?" Paul asked.

Chapter Fifty-Six

Natalia glanced one last time around the site. She feared this would be the last time she would see Göbekli Tepe. *So much pain here, so much terror,* she thought. She turned and climbed the steps to the VTOL aircraft. She gave a note to the Captain and said, "Please transmit this message to General Sullivan on this frequency… only this frequency. Once that has been done, take me to the Capital; have a car ready for me, and Tim Shaw should be notified to meet me there with a security detail."

"Yes, Ma'am."

*****

Some hours later, after making several copies of the data from a 3D laser scanning device and giving a copy to Sullivan, Tim Shaw held the car door open for Natalia. "Things are moving pretty quickly, aren't they?"

She smiled and nodded, "Yes Tim, they are and they are only going to move more quickly now."

Chapter Fifty-Seven

Mayor White answered, "Well, when something broke we had to fix it. If we couldn't we simply stored the broken gun in hopes that as we got better at repairs, we could salvage it. Now, we have folks that do nothing but repair broken parts and broken firearms. We've gotten pretty good at it.

"Reloading equipment gave us a chance to keep ammunition available, of course all of ours is charged with homemade black powder. In fact, we have learned that while more dangerous, black powder actually had some advantages. Doesn't work real well in semi-automatics but we have really good performance on pump shotguns, hunting rifles and revolvers.

"Often we would find books, most fell apart due to acid in the paper but again some were properly sealed and were still good. Some of our ancestors became scribes, laboriously copying the words before the pages they were on fell apart. Those ancestors saved astronomy and math for us. We learned science and medicine. From the Farmer's Almanac we learned how to read the seasons and keep farming.

"We found some seeds would not reproduce but others did. We found that some crops that used to grow here would no longer and others thrived. It became a question of doing the best with what we had until we could improve our situations. We studied windmills; repaired some and built more... we harnessed the wind and had power.

"With an understanding of gears, levers and other simple machines and us-ing horses, mules and cattle, we had power tools. We were satisfied with relearning old knowledge and eventually we began discovering things that others had discovered centuries before. We survived, therefore we were able to learn, improve and evolve our methods.

"Most did not survive, our ancestors did. We had some knowledge others did not. From the scraps of information and data we had we were able to postulate facts that moved us far ahead of the greatest minds of the past. Fourteen years after we had perfected black powder manufacturing on a large scale, we developed smokeless powder. The one thing we have never been able to perfect is reloading rimfire cartridges. All of our ammunition is therefore, centerfire.

"In our searches, sometimes we would find rimfire firearms. We have a whole warehouse of them, over seven hundred years old, in perfect condition, but no ammunition.

"We'll fix that for you," Paul said with a smile. "You said you have military weapons and ammunition; how did you come by them?"

"After a while it became necessary to send out hunter teams. Their job was to search for caches like what I'm talking about. Most of the time they'd come back empty headed, but not always."

"How far out do they go?"

"Depends mostly on the men and their horses; the hunter teams are usually five or six riders on good horses with supplies for three to four days. While a well-conditioned horse can cover one-hundred miles in a day, that's too much to do day in and day out. You'll kill the horse. So anywhere from fifteen to thirty miles a day is a realistic number to work with, depending on the terrain and the weather. Once the hunters have found a stash, we send a team of wagons to bring it back.

"One of our biggest hauls took place about six years ago. About ninety miles from here, to the east, is an old military installation called Fort Leonard Wood. Or, I guess I should say, what remains of it. We had heard a legend of a cache of hidden weapons. Allegedly, immediately before and just after the bombs fell on The Night of the War, a group of soldiers had been organized and began moving supplies into a cave nearby.

"We finally found the cave along the southern boundary of Fort Leonard Wood in the bluffs above the Big Piney River. We learned it used to be called Miller Cave and was part of a cave complex. We'll never know for sure but I suspect someone realized that the war was about to happen and there was no time to move the munitions to a safer place. They just tried to make sure the Russians didn't get them. At least they succeeded at that.

"There were cases of rifles, handguns, ammunition and special weapons... we also found twenty-four bodies sealed in the cave. We figure that when the

129

nukes hit St. Louis, fault lines all over the area shifted and part of the roof fell, killing the soldiers and sealing the cave.

"We only had two wagons available so it took almost two months to bring everything back. We didn't really know how to use most of the stuff so we just stored it."

*****

"What do you think of Mr. White, Wes?" Paul asked.

"Very unusual man," Sanderson said thoughtfully as they walked. "I would suspect a lot of his opponents probably have made the mistake of underestimating him. I suspect he can be both generous to his friends and diabolical when it comes to exacting revenge on his enemies."

Paul nodded. "White described himself as a devout Christian fundamentalist more than mainstream in his beliefs."

"Yeah," Sanderson said with a frown. "I think he can be a problem for us."

Chapter Fifty-Eight

"How long had your people been here mining the ἀμβροσία?"

Hundreds... of... generations... of... your... people. The... ἀμβροσία... never... disappeared... we... would... take... it... and... it... would... grow... again. The... supply... was... endless... our... people... prospered... as... never... before. Then... this... world... became... unstable... it... was... younger... than... my... own. We... thought... we... might... be... able... to... assist... the... Others. We... showed... them... things... they... had... never... known. What... you... would... call... science.

For... many... generations... the... relationship... was... productive... for... both... peoples. Some... of... our... science... was... impossible... to... teach... to... the... Others. The... minerals... on... this... planet... were... not... like... the... ones... on... my... planet. But... they... learned... and... they... learned... quickly... very... quickly. For... many... generations... there... was... harmony... between... my... people... and... the... Others. That... changed... when... the... one... known... as... the... Captain... came... to... power.

Rourke was stunned. "You knew the Captain?"

Yes... he... led... the... Others... against... us. He... attacked... us. He... destroyed... everything... including... the... means... we... had... to... transport... the... ἀμβροσία. Many... of... our... processing... locations... were... destroyed... by... the... battles... and... the... geological... shifts... that... occurred... when... this... world... shook... itself. Many... land... masses... disappeared... others... appeared. Finally... there... were... only... three... remaining… locations. The... supplies... of... ἀμβροσία… were... reduced... to... almost... nothing... and... it... became... necessary... for... us... to... ferry... it... back... to... our... world. Even... at... the... speed... our... vehicles... can... travel... the... distance... is... great... and... much... time... was... lost.

Chapter Fifty-Nine

"They kilt him, Mr. Mayor, they kilt my boy."

White took a deep breath. "Hiram, they say you and your son were firing at them."

"We never saw no one like them before, Mayor. You're always preachin' to be careful, stay alert, protect our town..."

Rubenstein interrupted, "We didn't even know your town existed. You attacked us for no reason."

A tear ran down the man's cheek. "I'm... I'm... sorry. I made a mistake and got my boy kilt. Now you're gonna kilt me..."

White motioned for Rubenstein to join him away from the prisoner. "Well, Mr. Rubenstein, I'd like to take my citizen home. After all, your people killed his son."

"Yeah, and his son killed two of our people and wounded another... with the help of your citizen."

White turned and paced for several moments before turning back to face Paul. "Hiram is one of the Toppers, the surface dwellers. He is a simple man; his fear of outsiders caused him to have to think beyond his capacity. So, exactly how do you see this playing out, Mr. Rubenstein?"

"I suggest you talk to Chief Sanderson, the dead and wounded were his men."

*****

Mayor White, Paul and Wes Sanderson sat at a table in the main tent. White smiled and said, "Chief Sanderson, what we have here is a mistake, a tragic mistake but still a mistake. You've talked to the prisoner... he is not, how do I say this?"

"He isn't the brightest bulb in the lamp?" Sanderson volunteered.

"Correct."

Sanderson nodded. "But he killed two of my men..."

White interrupted, "No, his son did and you killed his son."

"The son did what the father told him to do and died for it." Sanderson's jaw was set.

White nodded. "Yes Sir. And that father will carry that guilt for the rest of his life."

Paul interjected, "Chief, Mayor White, we have a problem to which I may have a remedy. Mr. White, we are under strict orders to keep the location of this site secret. The only way to do that now appears to be preventing you and your citizen from returning to your people."

White's eyes flashed hard.

"Chief, I'd like to speak with you privately," Paul said. Sanderson and Paul stepped away for several minutes then sat back down with Mayor White.

"However," Paul continued, "that has its own moral and ethical considerations. Additionally, since your people have discovered this location once... it is logical to assume it could happen again at some time in the future. Ergo, if it is impractical to keep our location a secret... it becomes imperative that we join forces to protect your people and mine. Do you agree?"

White leaned forward, "I suppose you are talking about a truce?'

Paul shook his head. "No, I'm talking about a temporary treaty between your town and this encampment. A mutual defense treaty that says each of us will come to the defense of the other if either is threatened by an outside force."

White leaned back in his chair and stared.

Paul asked, "How many citizens does Fanton have?"

"Just over a thousand."

Paul nodded, "None of whom are soldiers, correct?"

"Correct."

"But you do have a wealth of military weapons and ammunition, just no experience in how to use them, correct?"

"Correct."

"So, if we agree to this treaty and vow to each come to the defense of the other and if my people teach a select group of your citizens the skills of war and your people share with my people the military weapons and ammunition you possess in order to more appropriately defend both our peoples against a future threat... Does that sound like a deal to you?"

"What about Hiram Wesson?"

"Hiram goes home with you, to be tried and judged by your people and if found guilty to be sentenced to whatever punishment your people decide on."

Chapter Sixty

My... people... suffered... greatly... and... we... searched... for... other...
worlds... that... contained... ἀμβροσία. There... were... none. Finally... after...
watching... your... people... slaughter... each... other... in... many... wars... the...
last... one... the... worst... we... feared... you... would... destroy... the... only...
world... capable... of... producing... ἀμβροσία. Your... people... were... approaching... the... level... of... technology... the... Others... had... before... our...
war... was... launched. We... had... to... save... this... planet... not... only... for...
your... people... but... for... mine... as... well. We... made... contact... with...
your... government.

"We have just recovered records of those meetings," Rourke interjected.

For... many... years... the... new... arrangements... worked... well. The...
transportation... of... ἀμβροσία... was... increasing... but... as... the... technology... of... your... people... improved... so... did... the... number... of... incidents...
where... your... general... population... was... becoming... aware... of... us.

"And that is when you became part of a myth for us. Aliens, UFOs... the
stuff science fiction was made of."

Then... the... same... character... flaw... that... infected... the... Others... began... to... manifest... itself... again. Your... people... are... prone... to... self...
destruction... there... is... an... element... of... greed... and... fear... that... is...
present... in... you... but... no... other... life... forms... on... this... planet. Finally... the... bombs... began... to... drop... again. We... feared... it... would... be...
the... destruction... of... this....world... and...we...abandoned... our... sites...
around... the... world... and... left.

"The Night of the War," Rourke added.

This... is... accurate. We... watched... from... above... the... planet... as...
rockets... carrying... humans... left... again... for... space. It... was... a... repeat...
of... when... the... Others... left. The... planet... shook. Land... masses... disappeared. This... time... the... atmosphere... burned. And... as... it... burned... all...
of... the... ἀμβροσία... was... destroyed... or... so... we... thought. We...
searched... and... searched... but... ἀμβροσία... appeared... to... be... gone.

Your... people... had... killed... not... only... yourselves... but... my... people... as... well.

"But nature found a way," John said with a slight smile. The creature gave what could have been seen as a slight nod of its large head.

We... came... back... many... times... and... monitored... and... saw... that... ἀμβροσία... was... growing... again. The... planet... had... survived... even... if... the... people... had... not. Then... we... saw... the... people... returning. A... desperate... race... began... collecting... enough... ἀμβροσία... to... save... as... many... of... our... people... as... possible... and... trying... to... locate... those... rockets... which... had... launched... when... the... war... started. We... were... determined... to... never... again... let... the... supply... of.... ἀμβροσία... be... diminished... or... destroyed.

By... the... time... we... returned... to... this... world... much... had... changed... including... the... climate... which... had... direct... impact... on... the... production... of... ἀμβροσία. We... had... only... one... functional... processing... location... left... this... one. But... we... had... brought... reproductions... of... the... rocket... people... to... serve... as... our... slaves... to... mine... and... protect... the... ἀμβροσία. We... captured... others.

"You used those of our people you cloned from the Eden Mission. You used them to attack us," Rourke said. "I was there; we captured some of them. You used mind control on them."

This... is... not... totally... accurate.

Rourke glared but the creature did not move. "Okay, tell me then, which parts are not accurate."

My... attempts... to... establish... contact... between... our... races... was... misinterpreted... by... your... people... because... of... the... Others... and... the... defects... in... our... reproduction... process.

"It failed because your clones were faulty? Is that what you want me to believe?"

Partially... but... that... is... not... accurate. I... speak... also... of... the... Others.

"The KI?"

The creature gave a slight nod of its large head.

"You once showed me an image of double helix we call DNA, the genetic map of my body and one for yours. Did your people modify the DNA of the Others long ago?"

No....

"Do you know if anyone or anything else did?"

I... do... not.

"Can you show me all three DNA sequences together? "Three double helix appeared. The Creator walked to one and pointed.

This... is... the... one... for... your... species.

The Creator walked to the second hologram.

This... is... the... one... for... mine. Finally at the last it said: This... is... the... one... for... the Others.

Rourke walked around studying the three rotating images. After several minutes, he turned to the creature. "They appear very close and the general structure is identical."

We... are... not... so... different... from... you. The... differences... are... small... in... comparison... to... our... similarities.

"But," Rourke's mind was spinning now. "How is that possible?"

It... is... simple. We... the... others.... were... created... as... your... species... was. The... same... way. We... and... all... sentient... life... forms. More... similar... than... different.

Rourke thought a moment. "You told me one time that your species believe that God was real and he had also created your people?"

God... that... is... accurate. All... peoples... everywhere.

"Then I need your help. I need your help to save this world for my people as well as yours. Plus I need your help to save the KI. Not all of them are evil, but they are being led by an evil man, as are the Russians."

All... peoples... all... different... all... the... same. We... each... world... each... individual... creature... chose... be... good... or... not... good. Our... choice. The creature gave what could have been seen as a slight nod of its large head.

"If we are successful, I promise you that we will do everything possible to assist you in finding and processing all of the ἀμβροσία your people will ever need. If we are not, it will mean the end of both of our peoples. I need as many of your crafts as possible, like the one that brought me here. I need all of them you have."

Take... the... craft... all... of... the... craft... save... three... Those... must... be... held... back... for... the... shipment... of... ἀμβροσία... to... my... home... world. You... must... begin... training... your... people... John... Rourke. There... is... not... much... time.

Chapter Sixty-One

The news flashed across the screens of every television and computer in every civilized country of the world. John Thomas Rourke had returned. He had been rescued from some, as yet, undefined set of circumstances that had a direct effect on national security. The relevant points were that Rourke was safe, whatever threats to national security had been eliminated or neutralized, and the country was celebrating.

What no one knew was that Fantastic Caverns had been discovered and was in the process of becoming the new Retreat. Paul, Akiro and Wes Sanderson had returned to the Caverns to begin Phase Two.

John Thomas Rourke's gurney was pulled from the back of the ambulance and rolled quickly into the secured Emergency Room at the Tripler Army Medical Center. Once inside, the entire first floor was surreptitiously sealed.

With a cover story of an accidental industrial chemical spill on the other side of town, the media had been successfully misdirected to that location. Tripler Army Medical Center had begun as simple wooden structures within Fort Shafter but now was an ultra-modern hospital and the largest in the entire Pacific Rim region.

Tripler had been chosen for its current mission not because of its larger floor space but the fact it could be sealed and secured to handle a classified and covert mission such as this. Secrecy was essential in these final days.

For the next several hours, John Thomas Rourke was again poked, prodded and examined as though he was a new specimen of science, which as the first documented human to have been captured and lived with an Alien species; he was.

Sunlight was beaming past the vertical blinds in John Rourke's hospital room. Rourke sat on the edge of the bed, fully dressed in combat boots, denim jeans and a shirt. His double Alessi shoulder holster with the matched Detonics CombatMasters lay next to him on the bed. He was putting the final edge on the green handled Lancer/ A.G. Russell Survivalist Sting Michael had given him after his rescue.

The feel was different from the black chrome Sting 1A he had carried for so long—but he liked the little knife. Wiping the blade on a paper towel, he slid it into the brown leather sheath and placed the knife just behind his left hip.

The door opened and Tim Shaw and Michael Rourke stepped through. "Hello, John. Glad you're back," Shaw said with a weak smile.

John stepped forward and took Shaw's extended hand. "Tim, I'm sorry I wasn't here... wasn't here to help... to do..."

Shaw grabbed Rourke's hand. "Wasn't anything to do, John. There wasn't anything more any of us could have done. Once the baby got sick... There wasn't anything anyone could do."

"Can I see Emma, Tim?"

Michael spoke, "That's why we're here Dad."

Tim pulled a folded sheet of paper from his inside jacket pocket. "John, Emma doesn't want to see you... not right now at least. She sent this to you."

John took the note and opened it:

My Dearest,

I am so thankful that you have returned safely. Please understand that the pain and shock of the past weeks and days have taken a terrible toll on me. I haven't slept or rested well since I lost you and the death of Wolfgang and certainly not since the loss of our baby.

Everyone has been wonderful to me, especially Sarah and Otto. Poor Sarah struggled with her own losses and then has been so kind to me. Michael, Natalia and Paul and Annie took very good care of me and you should be proud of them. Paul is away right now but I know that Natalia and Annie need to see you as do all of the kids, I'm sure they can't wait to see you.

John, I love you so very much... I can't expect you to understand... I can't understand it all myself but I can't see you right now. I want to... but I can't... Please try to understand and forgive me.

I need a little time to sort out things in my own head.

Know that I love you with all of my heart.

Emma

John stood silently as he slowly crumbled the paper with both hands.

Chapter Sixty-Two

Colonel Sergeyevich went first to his quarters and encoded a message to his headquarters. It said simply, "It is time." Then he went to the Command Section of the ship and called a meeting of the KI fighter pilots. "Gentlemen, the Captain has given us permission to initiate the final stage of our plan. Squadron leaders, contact your counterparts on the other ships and convey that information. I wish to have a status report on the operational capability of all squadrons from all ships within the hour. Dismissed."

*****

General Rodney Thorne in The Egg observed the aircraft below him. The squadron consisted of two flights, designated Red and Blue. The formation was called the Four Finger. Each flight consisted of four aircraft, composed of a "lead element" and a "second element," each of two aircraft. When viewing the formation from above, the positions of the planes resemble the tips of the four fingers of a human right hand, minus the thumb, giving the formation its name.

Four flights—in this case, Red, Blue, Yellow and Green—made up a combat squadron. This formation had been used by many air forces since before World War II. It is the one usually associated with the Missing Man Formation at a pilots' funeral. The formation performs a fly-by in level flight over the funeral, where the second element leader climbs vertically and departs the formation, symbolizing the departure of the person being honored.

0		0	
Flight Leader - Commander Kuriname		Flight Leader - Commander Billings	
Eden Project		Eden Project	
0	0	0	0
Flight Wingman	Element Leader	Flight Wingman	Element Leader
Lt. Hayden	Lt. Washington	Lt. Johnson	Lt. Carlton
Eden Project	Eden Project	Eden Project	Eden Project
	0		0
	Flight Wingman		Element Wingman
	Capt. Daryl Dickinson		Capt. Hank Storm
	USAF		USAF

Jerry Ahern, Sharon Ahern and Bob Anderson

The lead unit is made up of the Fight Leader at the very front of the formation and one Wingman to his rear left. The second element is made up of an additional two planes: the Element leader and his Wingman. The Element Leader is to the right and rear of the Flight Leader, followed by the Element Wingman to his right and rear.

Both the Flight Leader and Element Leader have offensive roles, in that they are the ones to open fire on enemy aircraft while the flight remains intact. Their wingmen have a defensive role—the Flight Wingman covers the rear of the second element and the Element Wingman covers the rear of the Lead Element.

Four of these flights can be assembled to form a squadron formation which consists of two staggered lines of fighters, one in front of the other. Each flight is usually designated by a color. It remained one of the most efficient combat formations around.

Instead of airplanes, there were a total of eight Eggs on semi-permanent loan from The Creator, plus the one recovered in the tunnel during the attack on the Waiāhole valley; nine in total with Thorne's Egg.

The lead element in the first flight was piloted by Akiro Kuriname; five of the others were piloted by one of the Eden Project pilot clones. Two were being piloted by Air Force combat pilots on loan from the Department of Defense.

Out of a total of thirty-four potential pilots who had begun their secret training several weeks ago, only these remained. Thorne was pleased but wished he had three times as many ready for combat. The only advantage they truly had was the Alien technology. Thorne himself had already defeated two unidentified craft that had been proven to be KI fighters.

The Air Force and Marine pilots had the most difficult learning curve; they were handicapped by their own training and combat experience. Thorne understood; he had already learned that many of the limitations of the jets he had flown were nonexistent in The Egg. Things like gravity and thrust-to-weight ratio didn't matter anymore. They had learned how to compensate. Thorne felt they were ready.

The two big questions he had no answer for were: Were the pilots of the two craft that had attacked him KI or Russian and... Did it make any difference?

142

Had he splashed the KI fighters because the Russians had not mastered the KI technology yet or were the KI fighters just not very good? The Keeper had confided that during their long journey through the universe, there had been no opportunity for combat training.

Thorne decided he probably would never know the answer to the first question and not to worry about the answer to the second question. *No sense in freaking yourself out over a question that you might not want to know the answer to. Time would tell, time would tell.*

The real issue was the KI Armada consisted of thirty-seven individual ships. Did each ship carry a compliment of KI fighters? Even if they just carried one ship each, Thorne's fighters would be outnumbered almost five to one. Not good odds no matter how you sliced it.

Suddenly another part of the equation leapt into Thorne's head. *Holy Crap! What if we have to fight the KI in the KI fighters **and** the Russian's in Russian fighters? How many Russians would be in a battle like that?*

What upset Thorne most of all was that he hadn't thought about this before now.

Chapter Sixty-Three

Following the second examination, John Rourke now waited, alone in a hospital room that felt like a prison. It had been arranged that he and his family would be separately traveling to the neighboring island of Maui to spend some alone time and recuperate.

On The Night of the War, a tsunami wave had destroyed the beautiful town of Hana on the eastern tip of Maui. The land had sat idle until a local land owner had donated it to the office of the President as a private retreat. Of course in return, he had received some lucrative defense contracts and the contract to construct the private retreat that over the years had provided a secluded place for negotiations with other heads of state and a relaxing break from the affairs of state.

The next day, John Rourke was secretly moved to the Presidential retreat in Hana on the island of Maui. With a beautiful white sand beach with lava rock access to the ocean, breathtaking island views, a private golf course, beautiful scenery, SCUBA diving and horseback riding; the place was gorgeous.

In Hana, John and Emma would try to re-establish contact with each other. Half a world away Roderick and Andrea were pulling resources together for an attack on the free world and the Rourke family.

Sitting on the deck with his feet on the rail of the porch, John wished there was more time... more time for healing. During his medical training, Rourke had been forced to go through one rotation in obstetrics, a medical specialty dealing with pregnancy, childbirth, and the postpartum period. He had done well enough but had not cared for the experience. It had taught him however, that grief is a normal process and includes a shifting of emotions such as denial, anger, bargaining, depression, and acceptance.

He was not a psychiatrist, like Dr. David Blackman, but he knew that post-partum depression was a complex mix of physical, emotional, and behavioral changes that happen in a woman after giving birth. According to the current manual used to diagnose mental disorders, PPD is a form of major depression that has its onset within four weeks after delivery. The diagnosis of postpartum depression is based not only on the length of time between delivery and onset, but also on the severity of the depression.

PPD was linked to chemical, social, and psychological changes associated with having a baby. The term describes a range of physical and emotional changes that many new mothers experience. The good news is postpartum depression can be treated with medication and counseling.

Symptoms of postpartum depression include difficulty sleeping, appetite changes, excessive fatigue, decreased libido, and frequent mood changes. However, these are also accompanied by other symptoms of major depression, which are not normal after childbirth, and may include depressed mood; loss of pleasure; feelings of worthlessness, hopelessness, and helplessness; thoughts of death or suicide or thoughts or hurting someone else.

Eddie was Emma's third child, but due to circumstances lately, Emma had had less social support, more time living alone and, with John Rourke's life-style, there was always some degree of marital conflict; three of the major risk factors for PPD.

He knew that losing a baby had to be the worst thing a parent could experience. There are no words to explain the depth of despair that a parent goes through when attempting to understand the shift that occurs when all hopes and expectations suddenly drop out from underneath anything stable.

He remembered the director of nursing had told him that many moms will experience depression that includes feelings of guilt, shame, self-doubt, and sometimes suicidal ideation. Regaining a sense of self, hope, and trust is important to one's healing after a loss such as this.

Grief felt after the loss of a baby or child is not necessarily depression and while there may be some overlap, it should not be treated as such. If you feel angry one day and dissociated from your loss the next, this is normal.

The director of nursing had told him, "Loss can often beget feelings of loss. Women who have lost their babies become suddenly afraid of losing everything else, be it their sanity, other relationships important to them, their faith in the world, or any hope for the future."

He realized that Emma had become increasingly isolated during this time. He had not been there to give her support; she had to be her own support. Even Natalia and Sarah had not broken through her wall.

Now she wanted him to understand what she had gone through and Rourke feared he might not. People grieve differently. Often, losing a baby is a very different experience for a mother than it is for the father. After all, she was the one who felt the development of this baby and feels, still, the physical loss as her body adjusts to no longer being pregnant.

Chapter Sixty-Four

"The issue is pretty simple, Mr. President," General Sullivan said. "You and your entire family have to die. Otherwise, whoever is directing this operation will continue to hunt y'all down. You will never be able to consolidate your forces and take the country back, much less the world. Your death has got to be absolutely world without end, confirmed. Not by pictures but by forensic science that is indisputable."

"Okay, Frank... Just how do you expect that to happen?"

"Been thinking about that and couldn't figure it out until I thought about how all of this got started."

Michael frowned. "Huh?"

"Captain Dodd attacked your father and stepmother while they were on the archaeological dive in the Mediterranean, remember?"

"Yes, but I still don't get it."

"Captain Dodd... Captain Dodd, Mr. President..."

"Suddenly it hit Michael. Understanding, he stood up and started pacing, pacing and thinking. "Okay, okay... this might work."

Chapter Sixty-Five

Rodney Thorne rushed into the room and shouted, "Saddle up!" He ran toward the formation of Eggs parked in the east tunnel. Moments later the nine birds were sealed tight, cloaking devices active and speeding down the tunnels.

In just seconds, they flashed out of the east tunnel and began climbing to attitude. Closing on them was a massive storm front; Thorne headed the two flights directly for it. "Okay, Gentlemen. This time it counts. We are going hunting, but remember we are also being hunted. Stay sharp, work together... we are outnumbered but we have them on technology. We also have surprise. They have been flying now for two hours totally unopposed.

"The Russian MiGs are pretty good aircraft but they cannot contend with these birds. The other advantage we have, I think, is that the MiGs and the KI craft are being piloted by Russians. The KI apparently have lent support to the Russians but are not willing to jump into the fray just yet.

"The KI have had a long time to learn their own craft, but it would be like us trying to teach someone else to drive an old stick shift car when all they had seen was an automatic transmission. Eventually, they do pretty good, but in the beginning, not so much. I have already come up against two of the KI craft and I have no doubt they were piloted by Russians. Otherwise, they would have splashed me instead of the other way around.

"We have ten bogies on the scope. Red flight, I want you four to make the initial attack. Blue flight... you provide cover. Blue flight, you engage as necessary. Wingmen I want you strictly covering your element leader."

Commander Landon Billingsly radioed, "Red Leader calling Overwatch, Excuse me, Sir, but is that four of us against ten bogies? Over."

"But you have the element of surprise and three friendlies to cover your butt. Over."

"Roger, okay Red Flight, combat maneuvering now, prepare for dog fight. Red 2 take your element to the right side of the formation. I'm hitting the left. Nail them quickly and head into the clouds after the first run. Blue Lead, you sweep up the rest of the trash and we'll cover you. If we splash them all on the first two attacks, form back up on me and we'll roundabout with Overwatch. Over."

Next came a series of acknowledgements and the single formation broke into four two man formations.

Red Flight Leader and his Wingman dived toward the left side of the ten ship formation. Firing in trickle mode, they cut through four ships before anyone realized there was something wrong. The Element Leader and Wingman on the right side smashed into the formation in repeated blast and burst modes. They wheeled right, climbed and dove again. Four more KI fighters disintegrated.

"Blue Flight Leader to Blue Element Leader, we have two running for home. They are headed into the storm cover. You take the right one, I'm on the left."

"Roger."

Seconds later, came the call, "Red Flight Leader to Overwatch. Can you confirm all bogies are down? Over."

"Overwatch to Red Flight Leader, I can confirm. Form up and let's head home. Over."

Chapter Sixty-Six

Five men walked toward the covered patio next to the white sandy beach, where John Rourke stood. This would be the first time they had met together alone since Rourke's return. Paul Rubenstein was darker than John remembered and bulkier through the shoulders; he looked... it finally hit Rourke. Paul looked older and he carried himself with a sureness John had not seen in a long time.

Michael looked older also, but his was one of weariness not age. There was a tinge of grey at his temples that had not been there before Rourke's capture. Tim Shaw looked the same; stubble on his chin had moved a 5:00 shadow closer to 8:00 p.m. His dark suit looked like he had slept in it, because he had. His son Eddie, however, was dressed in starched and ironed Black BDUs that had S.W.A.T. over his left breast pocket and SHAW over his right.

Otto Croenberg was the only one that looked unchanged. Dapper and dangerous, lean and lethal; the pulsating vein on the right side of his bald scalp was more evident than usual.

Rourke knew how he looked. After all of the months spent with the Creator, he was paler than normal and with recent exposure to the sun, tinged red with slight sunburn.

Eddie Shaw keyed the microphone attached to his shoulder and said simply, "Tango, over."

There came a response of, "Bingo, out."

Shaw said, "We're secure John."

Rourke nodded. "First of all I want to thank each of you for what you have done to take care of the family while I was... away. I know how I feel after just the last couple of days, but each of you has been dealing with issues the whole time I was gone. Each of you..." Rourke was at a loss for words and his eyes were stinging and he looked away.

Otto filled the awkward silence. "You would have done the same for any of us, John. You're welcome and now let's get down to business, shall we?"

John looked back, smiled and said, "Right. Paul how goes the new Retreat?"

"The Retreat is habitable now but we're not finished. The longer we have the more we can do... we need as much time as we can get for maximum effectiveness. But if we had to go in tonight, we could."

"Michael, you and Paul came up with this idea. How does it look from your side?"

Michael was sitting on the edge of his chair, leaning forward, his chin resting on one fist supported by his right knee. "Two phases to this dad, well... actually three. The first was location. Paul, Akiro and Sanderson's Marines found the place and it is secure. Paul pulled all of the required equipment I wanted out of the first Retreat and it is all in place. Phase One is complete.

Phase Two is stocking the new Retreat with all of the logistical supplies we can and creating a structured environment that will sustain our forces. That is still underway, but honestly... I doubt we have enough time to finish. It was forecasted to take at least three months and we're just now at a few weeks at best. Close but no cigar."

At that comment, John Rourke stood up and said, "My apologies..." He opened the cabinet door near the outdoor oven and pulled out six rock glasses, a bottle of Seagram's and a box of cigars and passed them around. "I've been somewhat distracted fellas." He pulled his battered Zippo from the watch pocket in his blue jeans, bit the end off of a thin dark cigar and spat it on the ground. The yellow blue flame was pulled into the end of the cigar and after three puffs the cigar was going to his satisfaction.

A sense of normalcy rather than chaos settled over the men. This was familiar. This was as it should be.

Michael splashed Seagram's in each of the glasses and passed them around, holding his up in a toast, he said simply, "To the family." Glasses clinked and Michael went on. "The biggest open ended situation is when do we pull the plug and how much damage control can we exert to keep others from suffering. That's Phase Three and I need some input."

John looked around but no else offered an opinion. "Okay, let's do a reality check. We are not going to be able to save everyone. According to conversations that Michael and I have had, he has kept the number of knowledgeable personnel far lower than I dreamed possible. The main issue has to be the safety and security of the family first. Any arguments there?" There were none.

"Michael, when is your mother going to be back from New Germany?"

"Two days."

John looked at Paul. "Then you have seven days from tomorrow to be finished at the Retreat. Michael, have your people increase shipments to the Caverns as much as possible without creating suspicion. Tim, I need you covering Emma right now. My absence has not been good for us and my continued absence trying to coordinate things is not going to make it any better."

Tim nodded. "Already figured on it, John. Between Eddie and I, we can keep the law enforcement and security plans coordinated and cover her."

Otto Croenberg raised his hand. "I have a suggestion my friend. If Sarah is not returning for two days, allow me to coordinate the situation concerning the return of the rest of the children from Camp Zero."

John nodded. "Thank you, Otto. Gentlemen, like that old song said, "We've got a long way to go and a short time to get there. Michael I need a meeting with Generals Sullivan and Thorne first thing in the morning."

Michael nodded. "Figured you would, it is set up for 9:30."

The rest of the evening was spent catching up on the details of what had transpired during John's absence. Far more had occurred than he knew of. He looked at these men and saw them in a new light. Always before he had been there to direct, to strategize, to plug holes and make things happen; hard things. For the past weeks, they had done it all and done it well. He was proud of them.

When he finally walked into the bedroom, Emma was asleep. Rourke slipped out of his clothes and slid into bed next to her. Lying on his back, he stared up wondering if his life would ever be sane again. A few moments later, Emma rolled over kissed his cheek and laid her arm across his chest.

Maybe, he thought. *Just maybe...*

Chapter Sixty-Seven

When Otto Croenberg arrived at Camp Zero, he was met by the new Director, James Oglethorpe. Croenberg was traveling in the guise of Herman Milligan, Deputy Director for Presidential Security. Oglethorpe was a no nonsense administrator that had no desire to have Federal representatives on his grounds any longer than necessary.

After the attack of the Starlings, the Rourke and Rubenstein children had become almost folk heroes to those that knew the story. It took about fifteen minutes to have the kids and their baggage loaded up. John and Emma's daughter Paula, and Paul and Annie's daughter Natalie, were both sixteen years old. Timothy, John and Emma's son, and John Michael, Paul and Annie's son, were both fourteen. Michael and Natalia's son, John Paul, was tall for his thirteen years and so was their ten year old daughter, Sarah Ann.

Once they were safely on the road, Paula said, "So, Mr. Croenberg, what is going on?"

Otto was taken back a bit that his disguise had been so easily penetrated by children; then he laughed. "Well Ms. Rourke, I have a surprise for all of you."

Timothy frowned and said, "This family doesn't need any more surprises right now." John Michael agreed loudly from the rear of the van.

Croenberg pulled over to the side of the road and turned to face the kids. "I'm pleased to announce that Paula and Timothy's father has been returned to all of us and he is in fine health." Paula started to cry and Tim put his arms around her. Croenberg turned back to the wheel and drove off.

"You had better be telling us the truth, Mr. Croenberg," Tim said, jutting his jaw out. "This is not something to make jokes about."

Croenberg nodded solemnly. "I assure you Mr. Rourke, I understand that and this is the truth. I wanted to come for you myself to help explain some things to you all. As I said, John Thomas Rourke is in robust health, sharp of mind and body, you might say. However, Mrs. Rourke, your mother, is still not well. I tell you this because I believe you have proven yourselves quite capable of responsible actions above your ages.

"Also, there are many things happening across all of the families right now, things that unfortunately will have impact on all of you. To be honest, I'm not sure what they all are, but I feel you are better prepared to deal with the unknown if you know that such a thing exists. Also, in fairness to your parents and aunts and uncles… I'm sure they don't have all of the answers either. Nor do they know how everything is supposed to play out or, for that matter, will play out.

"As I said, I have found each of you to be resourceful and courageous over the past months. I would like it if all of you would do me the honor of thinking of me as a friend, even a confidant should you need one. Things will be somewhat unpredictable for a while. If I may be of service to any of you…"

The rest of the trip was spent in hushed tones and the Rourke/Rubenstein children tried to anticipate their future. Two things they all agreed on were that they were glad that John Rourke was home and they were anxious to see their families again. Whatever the future brought they wanted to face it as a family.

Chapter Sixty-Eight

At the Presidential Retreat, John and Emma's two children rushed into the room. Emma slowly followed; she sat on the couch and allowed Paula and John Michael the chance to visit their father. After about ten minutes he said, "Guys, why don't you get settled and let me have a minute alone with mom." They grabbed their bags and headed to find their rooms.

John went into the kitchen and returned with a bouquet of summer flowers: daffodils, freesia, hyacinths and tulip bulb flowers, but mostly daisies. Smiling he said, "Hello Emma, I hope you like these. The florist told me there is nothing sweeter than a bouquet featuring cheerful daisies in one of his sunny yellow keepsake pitchers." He looked down at the floor. "I am so sorry I wasn't here for you."

Emma took the flowers John held. "Thank you..." She said it more as a question than a statement. More like, *Is that, what I'm supposed to say? Is this what I'm supposed to do?*

John walked over to her and held out his arms; she walked into them and he enveloped her. *She is so thin*, he thought. *So fragile.* He held her gently but it was like she wasn't there. *No response,* he thought. *I might as well be holding empty air.*

"I am glad you are home John," she said almost vacantly. "I really am, but I need to lie down for a while. Is that alright, for me to lie down for a while?"

"Certainly," he said. Rourke knew Emma felt a deep loss and grief and that those feelings were appropriate. He told her, "No one gets to tell you how you feel except you. Do you want me to sit with you?"

She smiled, slightly. "No, no silly... no sense in you sitting there watching me sleep. Relax, unpack... I just need a short nap."

John Thomas Rourke watched her turn and walk slowly down the hallway to their bedroom. She opened the door and walked inside and slowly the door closed. When the door latch snapped into place it sounded like a pistol shot in his head.

He felt empty. He had felt that feeling three times in his life: twice long ago and once not so long ago. He poured himself a splash of Seagram's in a rock glass and found Paula and John Michael; they talked well into the night.

Chapter Sixty-Nine

The next day Emma seemed better; not very animated, but she was talking. "Everyone has tried to be very supportive. It is not them... it is me. I feel hollow... empty. I don't really feel much of anything. It's like I can see what others are feeling. Some people's insecurities and fears keep them from being there for me, I feel sorrier for them than me." Rourke had said nothing.

"I get hit with a wave of sadness and despair when I least expect it. I find reminders in the places where I least expect them to be. I see a pregnant woman, or a baby or a playground or ads for baby stuff and I lose it, even when I feel strong."

He reached for her hand, he felt her start to move her hand... but she left it there. "Sweetheart, that is normal. People don't always know what to say. Some people will worry that bringing Eddie up and your loss in conversation will be upsetting to you. At the same time, you may want desperately to talk about him, to bring him to life through your words and memories, to make room for them in conversation and in your experiences. That helps to move on."

"I don't want to 'move on.' I don't want to have another baby. Even if I did have the desire, I'm afraid Eddie would be forgotten and I can't do that."

Chapter Seventy

Paula Rourke made a point of sitting next to Otto Croenberg at supper that next night.

Just before dessert, she slipped a note to him. It read: "If you meant what you said in the van when we were coming home about us doing the honor of thinking of you as a friend, even a confidant should we need one, meet me on the patio tonight at midnight. We need your help!"

Croenberg read the note quickly and without hesitation glanced at Paula and nodded. She nodded once in return.

*****

When Croenberg arrived a little before midnight, he parked his car a block away and scrutinized the area. Shortly after the assassination attempt on Sarah and Emma, he had determined that he needed a predictable but undetectable method to penetrate the security parameter around the Rourke property. He came up with an idea he was rather proud of but had to wait several days to implement it.

On the day his frustration was at its peak, an opportunity manifested itself. William Jacobs, senior supervisor for the utility department, had an accident while on duty during the swing shift. A section of floor he was inspecting in a new work area gave way. The accident was covered by the local television station and reports from the hospital stated Mr. Jacobs was in critical condition.

He drove to the senior supervisor's office wearing the disguise of a city utility worker. Luckily for him, and unluckily for Mr. Jacobs, everyone was at the hospital waiting on word of his injuries. Otto Croenberg picked the lock, entered the office and rummaging through the desk found the supervisor's repair log book. Scrawling Jacob's handwriting took only a moment of practice and Croenberg had issued orders placing a city utility monitoring truck at twenty-four rotating locations in a twelve block area, for the purpose of monitoring for gas leaks. This area had possibly been damaged in a recent shift of the bed rock as a result of the Kilauea Volcano.

This was to continue until further orders from Professor Jerome Morrell's office. Croenberg phoned Morrell and explained the need for such a ploy and Morrell agreed to play along. Each of the twenty-four locations had been specifically plotted by Croenberg to give him a quick and surreptitious accessibility to a path that would carry him to John Rourke's property. That property was located in the center of the twelve block area.

The security detail around the property was obvious but he knew where a single weakness in the parameter was tonight. The city utility vehicle was parked in such a position as to block the normal parking place of the security detail vehicle. It was just a slight change, one that garnered only fifteen feet of obstructed view to a hedge row that led to three back yards that backed up to the beach, that had a stand of trees blocking view. He moved through the hedge row, jogging through the stand of trees, taking a final look around and vaulting a fence, standing, facing the Rourke/Rubenstein children gathered on John's patio.

Paula held her finger up to her lips in the universal sign of "quiet" and whispered, "Thanks for meeting us."

Otto, whispered, "I'm honored that you trusted me. How may I be of assistance?"

Paula turned to her brother, Tim. "Show him."

Tim pulled an envelope from his shirt pocket and opened it, pouring the contents on the patio table; six black feathers and one white one fell out. Croenberg picked up each and examined them. "I see," he said. "You believe that the Starlings are still on your trail, I take it?"

Paula and Tim nodded. "Natalie," John Michael said, "each of us received one of the black feathers after we returned home. John Paul received two: one for him and one for Sarah Ann."

John Michael smiled. "At least they have the decency not to terrorize her directly."

Paula said, "Tim and I each received a feather the same day. In my envelope they had included a white one. I suspect they are taking credit for Eddie's death. With that Croenberg studied their faces. "And I assume you have said nothing of this to any of your parents, correct?"

Sarah Ann spoke for the first time, "Can I just call you Uncle Otto? I can't pronounce your name?"

Croenberg smiled. "Of course, my child."

Sarah Ann took a deep breath, "Uncle Otto, bad people are trying to hurt our family and us. Our moms and dads are doing their best to protect us, but they have to protect themselves also. Grandma Sarah has told us that you are a true friend of ours, is that right?"

"Absolutely, my child. If your Grandmother said it, it must be true."

Sarah Ann nodded, her face serious. "Okay then, we need some help. The others say everything is going to be okay, but I'm scared." A single tear rolled down her left cheek. "Can you help us?"

Otto Croenberg, as hard a trained killer as the world has ever known, felt the earth slide under him. He started to speak but could not. Clearing his throat, he finally said, "I make each of you a promise. As long as I am alive, for someone to get to any of you... they will have to pass through me. Many have tried that before, no one has been successful. Do you understand?"

Paula spoke, "My dad has told me that you are a very good man that has been a very bad man."

Croenberg nodded. "Your father spoke the truth."

Paula nodded. "No apologies or explanations?"

"None, your father spoke the truth. Remember, he said that I *was* a very bad man, not that I still am."

Paula looked around at the faces of her brother and cousins, each one nodded. "Okay, now you are Uncle Otto for all of us. We need your help, not that we do not trust our parents, but they need your help also. Bet you never thought you would have this many nieces and nephews, huh?"

Croenberg looked down at the ground for a moment, hiding a tear. Masking the moment, he looked up quickly, smiled and wiped his face, "No... no, I did not expect this. But, I am honored you have accepted me into the family." He smiled and thought of Sarah Rourke. "Fear not, Uncle Otto is here."

Chapter Seventy-One

Paul Dunlap, Michael Rourke's Press Secretary, was fielding a barrage of questions from reporters.

Agnes Briggs from Honolulu's largest newspaper, World Associated Press, asked, "Is it true that the President is suffering from a medical condition? He has not been seen in public for days?"

Dunlap simply shook his head. "No it is not."

"Then, Mr. Press Secretary, is it true the President is suffering from a psychological condition as discussed by Congressman Greene?"

Dunlap took a sip of water. "No Agnes, it is not true. That is simply another in a long line of speculative and inappropriate misdirections from the Congressman."

Bill Nolan, national political anchor for DOT, Dead on Target Television, asked, "Paul, we have reliable information that some kind of a covert military mission has been launched somewhere in the Arctic? Can you confirm this?"

Dunlap shook his head, this was the question he had been waiting for; the actual reason for the Press Conference. "Well, Bill, I think your information is not as 'reliable' as you think. Is that a military mission—no? This was a coordinated archaeological mission from the Mid-Wake Scientific Institution and headed by Dr. Jerome Morrell to examine artifacts that ARE located in the Alaska region, near the old Denali National Park.

"Due to the extreme weather conditions, President Rourke thought it a good idea to have military participation to protect the scientists. As it turned out there was already a Cold Weather Training Exercise planned, so it was not a serious issue to coordinate. Thank you ladies and gentlemen."

Dunlap turned and exited the room; shouts and questions chased him down the hallway until the door to the White House Press Room closed.

Chapter Seventy-Two

Frustrated, Delervello said, "Let's play a game, General Sullivan. Let's say, for argument's sake, that if the Aliens were responsible for the Night of the War, because Earth's major powers did not dispose of their nuclear weapons, how does that jive with our colloquial view of Colonel Vladimir Karamatsov? We have evidence that he manipulated the Soviet Union into initiating World War III, through a rogue faction of Karamatsov's KGB Elite Corps."

Sullivan nodded. "Karamatsov always had nefarious plans... He once said that 'But some few of my faithful I would sing their names in the pages of history.' We know he had plans to survive along with some of his KGB Elite Corps and be resurrected in time to take out the Eden Project before it landed. Fortunately, he died but that bastard, Colonel Nehemiah Rozhdestvenskiy, kept working the plan and would have pulled it off if John Rourke hadn't capped him.

"We know little of those 'few' survivors of the Elite Corps. There was a Major Nicolai Antonovitch that was promoted to Colonel and a Captain Andre Popovski that Natalia Rourke described as tall, thin and young, even though she had known him five centuries ago."

Delervello said, "There was an unnamed Major described as '... one of the survivors from before the Night of the War, one of the original men from Vladimir Karamatsov's KGB Elite Corps.' I suspect this major could have been Popovski, with a promotion from captain to major. Natalia Rourke is quoted as saying, 'He was a decent man who tried to warn me about the depravities of Karamatsov. From reports on him, he seemed capable enough and he could have staved off defeat for nine days after Antonovitch shut down the power grid and was killed for it.

"As strange and improbable as this theory might seem at first glance, re-member... John Rourke, his wife, son and daughter, Paul Rubenstein and Natalia Rourke, all made a similar five hundred year sleep to survive the end of the world. We know some of the KGB Elite Corps did also.

"What we are not sure of is, was there a second sleep like the Rourke group took for another one hundred and fifty year jump into the future? And if so, what happened to those individuals? Is there another secret base? Did they awaken from the second sleep when the Rourke's did? Could they still be asleep waiting to be awakened? If they did awaken, are they the missing factor in this equation?"

Sullivan nodded. "You're saying if the Rourkes could do it.... the Russians could have also."

Delervello smiled. "Exactly, and if that is true it would be a logical next step to assume they are either still aligned with the Aliens or are in fact aligned with the KI." He paused for a moment. "Hell, I suppose it is even possible they could be aligned with both groups for some purpose we have no clue about."

Sullivan frowned. "Then with the new information Natalia Rourke recovered from Göbekli Tepe, I think it is reasonable to assume that some degree of influence from the Russians, coupled with a belief on the part of the Aliens that we could not be trusted, probably took place. I think it is not a matter of which theory is right... I think it is a situation where both theories have a degree of applicability.

Chapter Seventy-Three

The Grand Hall stood empty, except for a tall woman dressed in white, Andrea. The fireplace had been lit and the heat from it was quickly clearing the chill from the room.

Knuckles knocked on the oaken door by the right side of the fireplace and Andrea opened it. "Colonel Mikhail Sergeyevich reporting as ordered, my lady."

"I am pleased to see you still have time for me, Mikhail," Andrea said, pouting as she traced the lapel of Sergeyevich's black uniform tunic. "I feared you were finding your pleasure with one of those KI bitches off in space."

Sergeyevich took her hand in his and kissed it. "Andrea none of those golden KI amazons could ever excite me the way you do. You know that."

Andrea jerked her hand back and snapped. "I await your report, Colonel."

Sergeyevich never tired of this little game of cat and mouse; one moment the seductress the next moment the dominatrix. "The mission is going as expected, Madame. Training of my men to pilot the KI craft is continuing at an accelerated pace. I expect them to be fully qualified by the end of the week."

"How many KI fighters are operational?"

"Forty-seven have been successfully converted to match your instructions. Work will continue on the rest while the operation is mounted. It is reasonable to anticipate some losses; we will have replacements if needed."

"Your men?"

"Ready and able and excited to complete the mission."

Andrea walked close to Sergeyevich's body, her breasts touching his chest. "I really like the way your uniform looks on you, Mikhail." She moved a strand of hair off his forehead. "I wonder what it would look like on the floor." Slowly she began to unbutton the tunic.

He reached for her and her hand flashed up in a stinging slap that stunned Sergeyevich. Her voice was granite hard, "You are at attention, Colonel." Sergeyevich's cheek was crimson from the slap but his eyes sparkled.

"Yes, Madame... my apologies."

"Tell me again, Colonel... what is your plan of battle?"

Sergeyevich cleared his throat and began reciting, "Upon orders from you or your brother we will launch all of the operational KI fighters. Four flights of ten fighters each will descend into the atmosphere with seven fighters held back in reserve above the planet. The first flight will target Europe and Asia. The second will descend to a position over New Germany and spread out to control South America. The third spread out to cover the Hawaiian Islands to control the continental American airspace and position themselves. The last will cover from Australia up through the western Pacific. In a span of just moments we will have complete control of all air spaces in the world."

"What about resistance?"

"We expect some, primarily from Mid-Wake and Honolulu. New Germany has a competent air force; however, we now control that government. Sporadic resistance from England and Spain, but the KI technology will make short order of them. I will be surprised if there will be more than token resistance from the western Pacific rim."

During his dissertation, Andrea's fingers had played along the front of his trousers, touching, stroking. Sweat was on Sergeyevich's upper lip. "All simulations indicate we shall have global air superiority within thirty minutes of launch."

"Excellent." Andrea breathed heavily as she pressed her lips to his chest. "And I assume we will have full satellite coverage to document this?"

"Yes, Madame. Andrea... I want you. Now..."

"You shall have me Mikhail. Not now but when you are victorious. I will be your slave... anything and everything you can imagine... this thing I shall do for you." She pulled down his zipper and reached inside. "But for now you will be satisfied with this, will you not?" She began stroking him and he moaned softly.

"Do you want me, Mikhail?"

"Yes... yes, I want you."

"Tell me what you want Mikhail."

He started to do exactly that... but after just moments his release came; sudden and explosive. Andrea removed her hand and wiped it on his uniform tunic. "Goodbye Mikhail, do not disappoint me. Do you understand?"

He zipped his pants, turned and marched out.

At the other end of the Grand Hall a panel opened in the floor-to-ceiling book case. Roderick stepped out, his face red and hard; his heels clicking on the hardwood floor. Roderick marched up to his sister and slapped her.

"You slut! I told you to stay away from that Russian bastard."

Andrea placed her hand over her reddened cheek and looked at the floor. "But brother, I simply want to insure his loyalty and that things go as planned... as you have planned."

"What you are insuring has nothing to do with my plans, just your sick pleasures. I have told you before... have your dalliances, do what you wish with whom you wish to do it with... but not here and not as a part of our plan. I will not allow you to tamper with what I have constructed." He grabbed her by the hair and jerked her head back forcing her to look into his eyes. His teeth were gritted as he whispered, "Do you understand?"

She tried to nod but he held her hair too tightly, finally there came a little whimpered, "Yes."

Chapter Seventy-Four

John Rourke went to the study and closed the door. He dimmed the lights then pulled his office chair away from the desk and sat down. He closed his eyes and started his relaxation exercise and slowed his breathing. When he felt sufficiently relaxed he reached out with his mind...

Keeper, it is John. I need your help and guidance. Nothing happened, there was no answer. *Keeper, can you hear me? Please answer. It is very important.* Nothing. He began his breathing exercise again. *Keeper...*

I'm here John. I was in a meeting with the Seneia. What is wrong?

Keeper, I fear things are about to go very badly. I know it will affect my people and my world and I think it could have impact on your people as well. I think it is important that we meet in person as soon as possible.

John, that is impossible. The Captain has totally restricted all travel to the surface. It seems as if weekly we have had more and more Russian ships and personnel arriving.

Was that why you were meeting with the Seneia?

Yes, John, we are all concerned about these developments, even those that were aligned with the Captain a few months ago are able to see that things have changed and not for the better. Not for our people and certainly not for yours.

Keeper, are you aware that I have seen the Alien known as The Creator?

Yes... I am.

Keeper, I believe there is much information that we have been using to make decisions that is... at best faulty and, at worse, completely false.

Hmmm, John, what are you speaking of?

Keeper, The Creator has shown me that it was not them, the Aliens that started the war that resulted in the KI leaving Earth. The Creator presented facts that support it was the KI that started that war.

John, do you realize what you are saying?

Yes... yes I do, Keeper. I am saying that if The Creator is correct, someone within the KI has deceived your people. I suspect that the militarized segment of the KI is to blame but I have no way of proving it. All arguments will come down to 'he said, she said' or in this case, the Alien said or the KI said. I have no idea how to prove either as truth and fact.

The Keeper was silent for several minutes. *John, do you trust me?*

Of course I do.

No, I mean do you REALLY trust me?

It was Rourke's turn to take a moment of pause. *I do.*

Then, John, I ask your permission to tap into your mind. With your permission. I must see what it is you saw when you were with The Creator.

Keeper, I don't understand, I asked you once if you could read my mind you said no.

Technically you are correct. We KI would find that type of contact repugnant, invasive and unethical. In one to one contact, such as this, your thoughts are your own. You must accept my contact and that contact does not allow either of us to pry. What I am talking about requires a minimum of three members of the Seneia: our Senate of Scholars and Philosophers.

Three?

Yes. One, like me, to make contact. Another member to add his power to my own for that deeper contact, and the third to maintain a safety factor to keep the two from taking control of the one, in this case... you.

Okay, I understand, but do you have two other members you trust to do this? And if the three of you accept this as fact... what do we do with that information?

Well, John, in that case... I suggest we act and act quickly. This will take some preparations on my end. I will need you well rested... let us do this in twenty-four hours. Is that acceptable to you?

Rourke was quiet for some time. *Alright, twenty-four hours from now, but again what do we do with that information?*

You cannot do anything with it. Only I can and I will need the support of the entire Seneia to do what must be done. It has been done only once before in the history of my people, it is called a kathairō. It means to cleanse. Be rested, this probing will be more difficult on you than our normal contacts. We will speak in twenty-four hours.

Wait... Keeper... but the connection had already been broken.

Chapter Seventy-Five

John Rourke thought about the time he had spoken at the conference of the International Council on Human Genome Research for the purpose of outlawing human cloning. "As you know there are three types of artificial cloning: gene cloning, reproductive cloning and therapeutic cloning.

"Gene cloning produces copies of genes or segments of DNA. Also known as DNA cloning, it is a very different process from the others. Reproductive and therapeutic cloning shares many of the same techniques, but are done for different purposes.

"Reproductive cloning results in living, breathing, thinking replicates of existing, naturally created animals. Therapeutic cloning produces embryonic stem cells for experiments aimed at creating tissues to replace injured or diseased tissues.

"Let's go back to reproductive cloning because it is the part about 'thinking' I have the most problem with. You see, ladies and gentlemen, I have been cloned. But while my clone was a perfect physical reproduction of me... the 'person' did not think like me. Possibly physically identical and mentally and emotional similar; but not identical.

"Should science replicate our bodies so that we can farm replacement parts for diseased livers, hearts, eyes, bones, skin? At one time that was what medical science was promoting. But in fact, therapeutic cloning totally eliminated that 'need." Why?

"If you replicate a liver or a heart from stem cells, that organ is alive... but it is NOT sentient. Sentiency indicates a 'sentient being'; is one who perceives and responds to sensations of whatever kind: sight, hearing, touch, taste, or smell. In other words, that creature is aware. Aware of its surroundings, aware of itself and, in the case of human clones, are made aware that they are replicates of other people; aware they are not 'real' people in the conventional sense.

"A mad man, a scientist name Deitrich Zimmer, created my clone as part of his plan to take over the world. My clone was willing to do that, but how can that be, you ask. Remember what I said a moment ago? While my clone was a perfect physical reproduction of me... that 'person' did not think like me. Imagine, if you will, a world in which you suddenly realize that while you are flesh and blood, you have awareness of yourself and your environment, but you are not a real person in the conventional sense. You are a copy of someone else. You are a counterfeit person, a duplicate, an echo, an emulate... simply a ditto. Whatever you want to call it, but you are not a 'real' person.

"We... we humans, we 'real' people often struggle with the reason for our own existence. Many of us suffer from a plethora of emotional maladies, mental aberrations and diseases. We at least can surmise that we are a creation of a more superior being called God. However vague and mysterious, that often translates to 'hope' that we were created for a 'reason.' Even a reason we cannot define.

"But if we were a clone, we would be a creation of man, not God. Imagine, if you will, a world in which your self-awareness cognates on the fact that you were 'made' by someone no more special than you. Then what happens if you meet your 'other self,' your original, your parent... what would the word actually be?

"This would not probably be your 'brother,' a benevolent friend... this would be the person that created you to grow body parts for themselves. You were created simply to extend that person's productivity or longevity.

"You, as a clone, would not have the same memories unless they also had been copied somehow and transmitted, implanted into your mind. So you are a false person, with false memories, false dreams, false history and false hope. I have not even challenged the question of when you create a clone, does that clone have a soul? I don't know, but I don't think so.

"You, as a clone, would not be conceived out of love, but created out of necessity or curiosity. You, as a clone, would not be conceived as a blessing, but created because someone chose to create you for their own purpose. While you and I may be moral beings with ethical standards... I assure you... we are in the minority.

"But a clone, however artificial, IS a being of flesh and blood. A clone, however concocted, IS a being that feels. A clone, however fabricated, IS a being that is aware... would you wish on any person or being the awareness that their existence was nothing more than a Petri dish science project? I met my clone, I saw into his eyes. I would not wish this... these feelings, this awareness on anyone or anything.

"I ask you do not allow this to happen again, ever again. I ask you not to allow, sponsor or support the creation of a living, breathing, sentient being. I ask you not to play God. I ask you to make human experimentation and cloning illegal; illegal now and forever."

Stem cell research continued, therapeutic research continued; reproductive human research was outlawed and all equipment destroyed. International support and treaties had kept human cloning experimentation buried with that mad man Deitrich Zimmer.

Now the very thing that John Thomas Rourke had fought so hard against and finally destroyed was the only thing that could save his family and friends.

Chapter Seventy-Six

Tim Shaw and Otto Croenberg sat quietly on the patio of Emma and John Rourke's home. The sounds of sea birds and crashing ocean waves drifted up from the beach. Shaw reached over and pulled the carafe closer and poured coffee for the two of them.

Otto took a sip and nodded thanks. "How is your daughter today, Timothy?"

Shaw grimaced; no one had called him Timothy except his mother and only then when he was in trouble. "I'm worried, Otto. It is like the spark has gone out of her... She just sits there in the nursery, alone."

"She is grieving, Timothy, but you know that. Grief is different for everyone, but you know that also. She is grieving for the baby in her way, and you are grieving for the baby and her in your way, but you..."

Shaw growled, "Yeah, 'but I know that.' She's a grown woman but she is still my little girl and there is nothing I can do to help her. I can't..."

Croenberg turned and saw a single tear creep down Tim Shaw's face. "No, my friend... you can't fix this for her but you can do something to help her. Be her father, not her friend... she has many friends but she has only one father and that is you. You are correct, she is a grown woman but she is still your little girl and right now your little girl needs her daddy."

Shaw sat back in the chair and looked at Croenberg for a long moment. Then he wiped his face with one hand and stood up, nodded and walked inside the house and up to the nursery where his daughter mourned her dead baby. He gently knocked on the door, twisted the knob and pushed inside. Closing the door behind him, he walked to the chair and taking Emma's hands in his own... pulled her to her feet... then wrapped her in his arms and squeezed so hard he feared he might hurt her. He held on.

It was in that moment the wailing began; she had cried many times since Eddie's funeral but they had been soft, gentle tears... Now they were hard, loud, wracking tears... She buried her face in Shaw's chest and struck his back with fury; he held on. She fought his arms, trying to pull away; he held on.

For long minutes the struggle raged through her heart, through her mind, through her soul; he held on. Tears of anguish ran down his face and dropped to the side of her face; he held on. Shaw noticed she was not striking his back but holding on to him. The wailing had stopped now and there was a shuddering as she fought to regain her breath. Slowly, her breathing calmed and the struggles eased. A quiet, little girl voice said, "I love you, Daddy."

Shaw smiled through his tears, kissed the top of her head and said, "I love you more, Baby Girl."

*****

Croenberg turned when the kitchen door opened and Sarah stepped out onto the patio. Croenberg stood, sat his coffee cup down and held the chair for Sarah to sit down. "Good morning."

"Good morning, Otto... I passed Tim in the kitchen. Is he alright?"

Croenberg thought for a moment. "No and yes... Timothy, like the rest of us, is struggling with the recent events, so... no. Timothy, unlike the rest of us, has focused on the one thing he can do right now to make a difference and he is doing that, so... yes."

At that moment, Emma's wails could be heard above the ocean waves. Sarah jumped up and started for the door. Croenberg grabbed her hand and stopped her. "No, Sarah... she needs him right now."

Sarah's face was pinched, her eyes red; she nodded. Croenberg looked at her for a moment and released her hand and stepped back. He did something he never would have imagined he would do. He held out his arms in invitation... Sarah looked hard at him, then her face softened and she walked into his arms and wrapped hers around him and cried.

Holding on to this strange man, smelling his after shave... she realized all of the pain, the fear, the anger... everything tied to Wolfgang's death, the loss of her adopted country, the loss of Eddie... all of it was beginning to leave through her tears. The crying became a sob, then a wracking sob and then... slowly... simply crying again.

Croenberg held her gently, chastely... feeling her body shuddering with her own pain and loss. He could feel her tears soaking into his shirt. He could feel her breath, ragged against his chest. He could feel... something he had not felt in a long time, stir in his own chest.

Chapter Seventy-Seven

The Keeper, or more accurately his holographic image, looked around the table; John and Michael Rourke, Dr. Jerome Morrell and General Frank Sullivan were waiting impatiently. John Rourke asked, "How long can you make this connection last?"

The Keeper's visage smiled. "Long enough, I assure you. I am with the Seneia; our Senate of Scholars and Philosophers. The KI society was always one based on intellect and physical strength. Our history shows that the KI had developed more rapidly than any of our neighbors. It was the KI who had developed population control to improve the person. Once genetics was discovered, it was only a matter of time before genetic engineering was realized."

Sullivan cleared his throat, "We need you to fill in some blanks for us. Nazism and Neo-Nazism ideology believed that the Nordic or Aryan races, thought to predominate among Germans and other northern European peoples, were at the top of a racial hierarchy. The Nazi official Alfred Rosenberg believed that the Nordic race was descended from what he called the Proto-Aryans who he believed had lived on the North German Plain and who had ultimately originated from the lost continent of Atlantis. Since we now know that Atlantis did in fact exist, it is probable that the Proto-Aryans were descendants of stranded Atlanteans."

The Keepers image smiled. "When the KI had left Earth, mankind was almost totally destroyed and humanity was reduced to just a few survivors using stone tools, clothing themselves in animal skins and seeking shelter in caves. Unfortunately, not all of the KI had been able to leave with the armada. Those that remained possessed knowledge of that destroyed civilization's wisdom, passing tantalizing bits, snatches of knowledge and tales of great exploits down through the ages as legend, myth and alchemy; they became legends that your forefathers morphed into Gods."

Michael added, "And demons..."

"Yes, demons and monsters."

"The Nazis felt that the Aryans were superior to all other races," Dr. Jerome Morrell added. "Aryan certificates were one form of official documentation that was required by the law for all citizens of the Reich. One required the owner to trace his or her lineage through baptism, birth certificates or certified proof thereof that all grandparents were of Aryan descent. Non-Aryans, like the Slavs, Gypsies and Jews were considered racially inferior and a danger to the German master race.

"Eugenic events where men and women... men and women of Nordic Aryans features... appeared on stage in swimsuits in competitions to be evaluated for their physical and mental qualities as marriage partners were common throughout Europe and North America in the 1920s. The Nazis took this concept to a further extreme by establishing a program to systematically genetically enhance the Nordic Aryans themselves through a program, based on laws passed by the state of California, to create a super race."

The Keeper gave a wry smile. "I now believe it is possible that the remnants of our people that were left on Earth when our armada left, could well be the source of the Aryan legend."

Chapter Seventy-Eight

The night little Eddie had been taken to the hospital, Emma had called him "Daddy." Tim Shaw had noted a definite down turn in Emma's mental state and attitude ever since. At times she was having memory lapses and times where she simply "phased out." She was there physically but mentally... Something had to be done so Tim Shaw did it; he had her admitted for observation.

Dr. David Blackman, Chief of Psychological Research at Mid-Wake, had completed his examination of Emma Shaw-Rourke. He checked his watch, still ten minutes before his scheduled meeting with her father, Tim Shaw. He made some quick notes and attached them to her medical record file and walked to the conference room to meet with Shaw.

"Special Agent Shaw," Blackman said.

"Doc, we are going to trip on all of the titles for both of us before this meeting is over. Let's just go with Tim and Doc if you don't mind."

Blackman smiled. "That works for me, Tim. Well, I have both good news and bad news, which do you want first?"

"Give me the good."

Blackman nodded and opened the file. "What your daughter has is called dissociative fugue. It used to be call a fugue state or psychogenic fugue. It is listed as a dissociative disorder in the Diagnostic and Statistical Manual of Mental Disorders. It is a fairly rare psychiatric disorder characterized by reversible amnesia of a person's identity, including that person's memories, personality, and other identifying characteristics of individuality.

"Doc, what the hell is a fog; and can she recover?"

Blackman cleared his throat, "Not fog; fugue and usually yes, and most of the time on her own. After recovery from fugue, previous memories usually return intact. Here is some of the bad news: there is typically amnesia for the fugue episode. In her case, the episode of fugue is related to external events, not related to the ingestion of psychotropic substances or to a general medical condition or to other psychiatric conditions. Her fugue was precipitated by a stressful episode, in her case two associated episodes. First the death of her son and second the absence of her husband. There appears to be amnesia for the original stressors called dissociative amnesia.

"Symptoms include mild confusion, and once the fugue ends, possible depression, grief, shame and discomfort. People have also experienced a post-fugue anger. We have carefully reviewed her symptoms and we did a physical examination to exclude physical disorders that may contribute to or cause memory loss. A psychological examination was also done.

"Luckily we were able to diagnose her now; sometimes dissociative fugue cannot be diagnosed until people abruptly return to their pre-fugue identity and are distressed to find themselves in unfamiliar circumstances. In those cases the diagnosis is usually made retroactively when a doctor reviews the history and collects information, that documents the circumstances before people left home, the travel itself, and the establishment of an alternative life."

"You are saying she could recover on her own, correct?"

Blackman nodded. "Yes, Tim, I think it is entirely possible. But remember I told you there was some bad news?" Shaw nodded. "The bad news is there is no way of predicting when, how or even for sure if that is possible.

Chapter Seventy-Nine

John Rourke realized he was alive. To sit up was impossible yet; he felt only the tickle of the electrical charge, the sensation of light touching his eyes, his eyes unused for five centuries and the sensation of the rising and falling of his chest.

There was no danger of falling asleep. But with his eyes closed, he felt his body awakening, never more aware of his body in so physical a way—it was like orgasm, only with the entire body as its focal point.

Alive...

Rourke sat up, the lid of the cryogenic chamber rising in rhythm with his body. He turned his head, he had been practicing that. The monitoring lights still glowed on the five other cryogenic chambers, still sealed. They too were alive: Sarah, Michael, Annie, Paul and his eyes rested on Natalia. He closed his eyes. She was beautiful even in her sleep as the swirling clouds of the bluish gas drifted across her face. But he missed the surreal blue of her eyes.

John Rourke looked to his right. His Rolex Submariner, he picked it up and as he did the sweep second hand started to move again. He would have to ascertain the correct time, the correct date. Slowly, not moving well yet, he placed the watch on his wrist and closed the flip lock clasp in place to secure it there; beside the watch, the twin stainless Detonics .45s.

He remembered now. There had been the fight with the last Soviet helicopter. He had killed Rozhdestvenskiy and Rozhdestvenskiy's submachine gun, it was an Uzi, Rourke recalled for some strange reason that it had fired from the chopper. The chopper had exploded and Rourke had dived for the escape tunnel. He remembered a wound to his left forearm, a rock chip. He had cleaned the wound, dressed it while he had gone about the rest of his business in preparing the Retreat.

The world had been dying outside. He had removed the bandage just before entering his chamber, just before injecting himself with the cryogenic serum.

The hypodermic needle, it lay on the floor beside the chamber now as he looked down. And he looked at his arm. The wound was healed and there was no scar. His pistols. Rourke had cleaned them, leaving them unloaded. He reached, picked up one of the pistols; the lubrication was still in evidence...

Suddenly, Rourke stopped. He frowned and looked at the scene closely. I remember this, he thought. I've done this before. I've been here before. His frown deepened; he squeezed his eyes shut, the muscles in his arms and hands tensed like corded steel. A growl began in his stomach... built in his chest and then exploded through his clenched teeth.

"NooooOOOOO," his jaws separated and the growl turned into a bellow, the bellow of a wounded animal. "The dream," he shouted in his mind. "This is where it all started. This is where my life ended. It was not the end of the world. It was when we awaken after the first sleep. It was before I made the decision to wake Michael and Annie and prepare them to survive."

*****

It had been a long time since John Thomas Rourke had dreamed this dream. He realized it had stopped when he met Emma. *Does this mean my heart or my head, or maybe both of them, believe Emma is lost to me?*

Chapter Eighty

Paul Rubenstein's satellite phone chirped, he looked at the number and frowned. "Hello."

"You saw the number?"

"I did. Then this is not an accident?"

"No. No, it is not. The timeline has shifted, we have to move quickly. How long before habitation is possible at the current rate of movement?"

Paul pushed the wire framed glasses back up on the bridge of his nose and looked around. "Not long I guess. The longer we have the more comfortable it will be, the more supplies we'll have, the better chance we'll have."

"Understood, I have some calls to make. Begin acceleration, we'll have to make do with what we have when it happens. I'll call you back with details." The connection was broken. Paul walked over to the edge of the cliff; he could hear the river below. He sat down on a log and looked back across the site and shook his head.

"Damnit Michael, we're not ready," he said out loud but to himself. We need a month, maybe two to do what we talked about." He looked at the satellite phone in his hand, stood up and shoved it into the pocket of his battered field jacket. He spotted Akiro Kuriname and Wes Sanderson standing together near one of the water storage tanks being moved into the cavern. He whistled and waved them over. He pumped his fist up and down and they looked at each other and broke into a double time.

"Guys, I just got a call from Michael. Something is going on and I don't know what but our timeline is about to be compressed."

"How bad?" Sanderson asked.

Paul shook his head, "Don't know, but you better light a fire under everybody. I'm waiting on a phone call from him with more details but I don't know when that will come... few minutes or a few days. I don't think it will be much longer than that."

Kuriname held out a clipboard and pointed. "Here's where we are right now. If an item is checked with (**X**) it is in place and functional. If there is a (/)

it is in place but has not been confirmed as functional. If there is a (\) it is in route."

Paul surveyed the clipboard. "Well, this is actually better than I thought we would be. How many more transports are we waiting on and can we do anything to get them here faster?"

Sanderson thought for a moment. "About eight more and if we change the schedule it will show up as a blip somewhere."

Paul studied the clipboard as he paced. Finally stopping he said, "Okay. Akiro, I want two squads of Dog Soldiers on close-in parameter security. Wes, I want three mobile squads of your Marines on distant security. I want active satellite coverage around the clock. Two hours on, two hours off for each operator. I don't want a robin or a rodent to get through our net without us knowing about it. Everyone else is to focus on equipment movement, installation and functionality.

"I don't know how much time we've got but we have to figure not nearly as much as we had fifteen minutes ago. I want our counter-illumination generators checked and rechecked. I only want one third of them operating at any one time with another third on standby and the last third in reserve. Wes, see if you can order more of them, we have to have spares to stay hidden."

"I'll try; how many to you want?"

"As many as you can get within raising suspicions." Both men saluted, turned and jogged off to implement Paul's instructions. He smiled and thought about that night so long ago in Albuquerque. The plane had crashed, he and Rourke walked naked through the streets, their clothes were contaminated with radiation and they were about to fight a pack of hungry wild dogs that wanted them for supper. He had been scared to death. Looking around he smiled and said in a soft whisper, "Yes, Mrs. Rubenstein... your boy turned out just fine."

Chapter Eighty-One

Paul Rubenstein rode Hiram Wesson's horse. James White rode his own and led the horse Wesson's son had ridden to the Retreat. The boy's body was tied across the saddle. Mr. Alexander and his son, Noah, rode their own horses. Behind them came three of the AATVs; Chief Sanderson in the lead with one guard and Hiram Wesson in handcuffs. Two escort AATVs each containing five of Sanderson's Marines; armed and ready.

Their arrival at Fanton caused quite a stir. As Rubenstein and White reined in their horses and stepped out of the saddles, the escort AATVs roared up next to them and the Marines bailed out and formed a security line. Sanderson pulled up next to Paul and White and exited the AATV; the guard and Hiram Wesson staying inside. White dismounted.

People were milling around confused, they had never seen anything like these vehicles or these men in uniform. One shouted, "Mr. Mayor... what is happening? Who are these men?"

White realized he needed a podium so all could see and hear him. Grabbing the saddle horn he swung back into the saddle and stood in the stirrups. "Ladies and Gentlemen, these people are our friends. There has been a terrible incident, Hiram Wesson and his son Billy attacked these people by mistake. Billy is dead. These people have helped me return Billy's body and bring Hiram home for judgment.

"I understand your confusion, I was confused also but now I need you to listen to me..." White continued his oration for another thirty minutes. "I am convinced that we should ally with these folks against an enemy that is approaching even as we speak. We don't have months to prepare, we may not have weeks, and we may only have days. There is much I still do not understand but what I do understand is this... Death approaches and he rides a pale horse. Our very survival may depend on what occurs here in the next few minutes."

*****

White selected an individual to escort Sanderson and three men to examine the store of military weapons and munitions that had been recovered from Miller Cave. Inside the underground they walked almost a quarter mile before coming to a group of structures that served as warehouses. Their boot steps echoed in the silence. When the large padlocks were removed and the doors swung open, one Gunnery Sergeant whistled and murmured, "Holy crap!"

Neatly stacked along the back wall were ammo cans from floor to ceiling and wall to wall; Sanderson could not tell how deep the stack was but he could tell there were multiple layers. They included 5.56, .45, 762x51 and 40 MM ammunition. Others held tear gas and smoke grenades.

Along the length of the left side wall were cases emblazed with Rifle, Caliber 5.56 mm, M16A1 and Pistol, Caliber .45, Automatic, M1911A1 and wooden shipping crates containing both rifle and pistol magazines, still wrapped and coated with Cosmoline. Along the length of the right side wall were cases that read: Grenade Launcher, 40MM M203 and Grenade Launcher, 40mm M79 and, United States Machine Gun, Caliber 7.62 mm, M60.

Sanderson smiled. "I see three cases for the M21 Sniper Weapon System and two of the M40 bolt action sniper weapon. One, two... five cases of Thompson submachine guns and two cases of the old M3 Grease gun." He turned. "Gunny, get me an inventory of everything and I mean everything."

"Roger, Chief."

Sanderson took off his cap and wiped the sweat from his face and head. He thought, *Right now things seem really right with these people. Why then do I have such a sense of dread?*

Chapter Eighty-Two

John Rourke looked around the table and at the holographic image of The Keeper. "I had several television shows that I considered 'special.' I particularly enjoyed the Lone Ranger with Clayton Moore, and Cheyenne with Clint Walker. Another of my favorites was a science fiction story about a spaceship that was on a five year mission. The timeline was several centuries in the future; I'll come back to that in a moment.

"One of the episodes was the first time that I remember actually hearing the term Eugenics. On the show, the spaceship encounters another ship whose crew is in suspended animation within cryogenic chambers. That ship was launched into space in the 1990s.

"That crew was selectively bred super people from earth's past; they were products of 20th-century selective breeding designed to create perfect humans; unfortunately they conquered over a third of Earth and became warlords. This was all fiction, except for the basic premise of selective breeding.

"In the late 1960s when this show aired, great advances were being made in technology and the next thirty years held great expectations. Unfortunately, imagination exceeded technology... Now, here in real time, almost seven hundred years have passed since that show aired…. birth control may well result in control of the population. The Nazis tried it after studying what law and policies were in place in America before World War II. Now, once again… effective propaganda has set the stage for destruction again."

"Why has it resurfaced and why now? "Michael asked.

John shrugged. "Why did Karamatsov, Rozhdestvenskiy and Dietrich Zimmer exist? There truly is evil in the world, physical and arcane evil. Michael, I told you once that had the Night of the War never come, it's sad to say that the eventual outcome for humanity might have been little different. The economy of the United States, like the economies of other nations, was already severely strained. The possible solutions to ecological concerns, such as the depletion of the ozone layer, global warming and over population, were staggering even to consider.

"The trouble," John continued, "was if anybody did know the answers, no one was telling. And that was just one of the problems facing humanity. There were diseases, there was poverty, there was international aggression; the catalog was almost endless. And fewer and fewer people wanted to be bothered by the problems. It was better to bury oneself in self-indulgence, bury the mind say in ephemeral pleasures and just wait for the inevitable cataclysm.

"Many people that were paying attention began to feel we all were being manipulated, like puppets on a string. The question was: Who was doing the manipulation and why? There were many suspects but since the manipulators, the Progressives, held sway over the news media, nothing was ever proven and the real agenda of many social experiments were purposely hidden from view.

"What are you saying the real purpose was? "The Keeper asked.

"To confuse and distract the population from the realities of the world. To keep the population so confused that the sanctity of life, the structure of the family, the practice of religion, the inalienable rights given to us by our constitution and God which could not be taken from us with violence... would be surrendered willingly because they no longer held value. To paraphrase T.S. Elliot, 'Mankind just went out with a bang rather than a whimper' the Night of the War.

"But man survived, but along with his greatness so did his pettiness, his baseness. I doubt that a blood line of the original Eugenicists still exists, but who knows. But what I do suspect is that somewhere, in the dark behind some curtain is someone who has been able to covertly coordinate a multi-level plan for world domination, one that does not require a single shot to be fired. Instead, self-indulgence will be the trigger and propaganda the weapon.

"What really amazes me is we haven't seen this before," Michael said.

"Maybe we saw it but just didn't recognize it for what it was," John said. "Hind sight is always 20-20, remember. Yeah, it was all sleight of hand, smoke and mirrors... hiding the facts, the true intentions. Rumors no one seems to listen to until suddenly someone's reputation is ruined; an insidious disease develops internally without symptoms, so that you don't realize right away that you are sick. An insidious plan proceeds without your knowledge and you don't realize you are in danger.

"You know, it is one thing to take a life when you are defending yourself, your family or your country. But that is different than taking a life because it is inconvenient financially or socially. How can you kill the innocent that can't defend themselves? First you dehumanize them with terms like fetus and embryo instead of calling them what they are... babies.

"Yes, and how much easier will it be one day to go after adults. If you dehumanize them with terms like the elderly, retards, cripples, druggies, kikes, gooks... the list goes on... instead of calling them what they are... people.

"Thousands of years ago, the Chinese philosopher, Confucius, said, 'If language is incorrect, then what is said is not meant. If what is said is not meant, then what ought to be done remains undone.'"

Chapter Eighty-Three

Earl Burger was working on one of the damaged computers when Paul Rubenstein walked by. "I thought you were primarily working as a medic for this group," Paul said.

Burger looked up and smiled. "There aren't very many of us on this team so we are all trained and crossed trained in different skills. That way if one of us with a primary skill gets taken out, others can step in and keep the team functioning. My primary is Advance Trauma Life Support but, like I said, I've also worked with computers for a long time. I used to do programming but my wife put a stop to that 'cause she didn't like the way I talked and acted when I was programming. She said I was like a cross between a robot and an android."

Burger took off his magnifying head piece and turned to face Paul. "I've heard about you guys and your immortality."

Paul shook his head slowly. "Immortality... hardly. We've just lived a long time. My chronological age, my biological age and my resurrected age vary greatly," Paul said. "Chronologically I am about 700 years old. Biologically I am almost 50 but my resurrected age... by virtue of two cryogenic sleeps shaves about 10 years off of that. Physically I am in the shape of an active forty something male.

"That is the good thing about all of the 'original Rourke clan.' John, Sarah, Natalia and I being the oldest, next is Michael and Annie, and then there's..." He stopped and looked down at the floor. It took a while before he could continue. "I'm still not used to Wolf being gone," he finally said.

"Wolfgang Mann, my friend, Sarah's second husband; he joined us before the second sleep. He had fallen in love with Sarah and when she was injured, he left the life he had in the hopes that one day she could be reawakened and they could have a life together. Now he is dead, killed by murderous Neo-Nazi bastards that attacked New Germany. Immortal, no—we're not immortal.

"Like Wolf, we can die. We can die from disease or injury just like every other person. We can be killed by a bullet, a knife, an energy blast or a car wreck. It has almost happened several times to several of us, but so far the universe has smiled on the Rourke clan. But..." he was again quiet for a moment.

"What's the matter?"

Paul looked up, pushed his wire framed glasses back on his nose and smiled. "Nothing, nothing really. I was just thinking maybe our luck has finally run out. Maybe this last mess will take all of us out of the game of life.

"If I'm not able to get the new Retreat ready and do it in time, if I'm not able to get the family and others in it... in time; we won't survive. At least not for long... and I'm not trying to sound egotistical but that could mean these bastards could take out the rest of humanity. Anyway, you keep an eye on things for me, Mr. Burger. I've been ordered back to Hawaii. Hopefully, I'll see you in a couple of days."

Chapter Eighty-Four

Rourke was closing now. "Look, we have to face facts. We have major catastrophes lining up on several fronts. Russians, probably surviving members of Karamatsov and Rozhdestvenskiy's elite KGB, have aligned with the militant KI. Neo-Nazis have quietly and carefully penetrated and, in some cases, have taken over the legitimate governments of many nations and seek to take over more. At least one manmade biological weapon has been launched against mankind and had we not been lucky, could have destroyed us all.

"We can no longer trust the media; we can no longer trust our politicians, if we ever could. We can no longer trust our institutions and I fear we can no longer trust our churches and synagogues. All we can trust in now is our God and ourselves and in what is right.

"The current set of circumstances is aimed directly at our most vulnerable; I have already lost a child I never saw to this madness. But rest assured there will be more innocent children to die and more weak and sick older people who will die. Because those two share one thing in common… it is in the beginning of life and at the end of life that a person is the most inconvenient.

"I know that there exists a hidden or shadow group that really is where the real and actual political power resides."

"You're saying it is not with our elected representatives?" Sullivan asked.

Shaking his head, Rourke said, "There has been a lot of speculation for a long, long time that there exists a group of private individuals, exercising power behind the scenes, beyond the scrutiny of democratic institutions. If so, the official elected government is really subservient to the shadow government who are the true executive power."

"Well, Michael should know, after all he was elected President," Morrell said.

"No, it is not that blatant, it is more subtle, more hidden," Michael responded. "I think it is possible that Phillip Green and even Peter Vale have no idea who they are actually working for. I think there is the residue of what we called a cabal that has reformed itself… or maybe it was never destroyed by The Night of the War. They certainly had the resources to structure their own survival. It is even possible they created the war for their own nefarious reasons.

"Before The Night of the War, the cabal had been attributed to the Vatican, the Jesuits, Jewish moneyed interests, the Freemasons but most usually to global elitists intent on creating a New World Order. That would certainly go along with the Eugenics movement and control of the population."

John Thomas Rourke turned to face the group. "The bottom line is this: To survive, sometimes it is necessary to sit quietly and watch and understand what is transpiring and respond, not react. A Roman, Tacitus, once said, 'He that fights and runs away, may turn and fight another day; but he that is in battle slain, will never rise to fight again.' Sometimes it is better to run away and fight another day. I think there is so much coming together at one time that we have no other choice."

Chapter Eighty-Five

Michael was sitting alone in his office with a pad and pen. He had been there for three hours putting the final touches on several lists of names—changing it again and again until he finally leaned back and said, "Okay." He scanned the list. It held the names of the people he trusted most in the government and military. Finally there were two lists of names. The first list was of those he trusted and would be able to safely remain. The second, those he felt were in the position to sacrifice the lives they had and disappear.

That meant extended families, careers... everything. It would be like entering the old Witness Protection Program the U.S. Marshall Service had created back before The Night of the War.

Michael looked at a printed note attached to a thick file; it said: Operation Phoenix. Below the title and in smaller type was a notation, "In Greek mythology the Phoenix was a long-lived bird, like an eagle only larger that begins a new life after rising from the ashes of its predecessor."

Chapter Eighty-Six

The Grand Archivist, Steve Delervello said, "I can say with very little hesitation that because Earth's major powers did not dispose of their nuclear weapons we, the governments of the planet Earth, found ourselves to be in violation of a contract. A contract we had entered into with an Alien species we had communication with for... well, truthfully... I don't know how long."

"Are these the same Aliens that the KI had dealt with so long ago?" John asked.

Delervello nodded. "I can't be sure but from all indications... yes. The Keeper believes they are one and the same. Their aircraft have been identified by both The Keeper and his colleagues. And yet again with the new information we have from the Mount Rushmore Vault of Ages, the evil Colonel Vladimir Karamatsov may well have manipulated the Soviet Union into initiating World War III. There is even evidence, although circumstantial, that there was a conspiracy even then between the Aliens and a rogue faction of Karamatsov's KGB Elite Corps."

"Karamatsov's people?"

"Apparently; I believe that one of his contemporaries, possibly a Nicolai Antonovitch, who is probably at least a Colonel by now. The other is a Major, possibly Andre Popovski, the connection between the KI and the Russians. The good news is we have someone that can identify him if Popovski is the connection; Natalia Rourke."

"What good would the identification do, just knowing who the bastard is that is working with the KI?" John asked.

"If it is Popovski and he remains the decent man who tried to warn Mrs. Rourke about the depravities of Karamatsov... we might have in fact an ally on the inside. Minimally, he might be able to confirm a great many of our speculations and questions. Like the legendary Third Chinese City that has been speculated on from the time of your first wakening. I think it is at least possible that the Third City is actually a group of Taoist and Russians somewhere along the Sino-Russian border. Not Taoist as we think of them today, probably a bastardized off shoot combination of Taoist and militant communist with political leanings from all the way back to Mao Zedong."

John Rourke shook his head. "Damn... Can't I ever get rid of Karamatsov? And now I'm looking at the potential of some of Mao's sick bastards."

Delervello said, "You have to remember, Dr. Rourke, as controversial figure as he was, Mao was regarded as one of the most important individuals in 20th Century world history. He was a theorist, military strategist, poet and visionary. Supporters credit him with driving imperialism out of China, and moving China into modern times and building it into a world power. He promoted the status of women, improving education and health care, and increasing life expectancy as China's population grew from around 550 million to over 900 million during the period of his leadership."

"Yeah," John said. "Well, he was also a dictator who was comparable to Hitler and Stalin. He severely damaged the traditional Chinese culture, perpetrated systematic human rights abuses and was responsible for forty to seventy million deaths through starvation, prison labor and executions. Sorry Steve, I lived in that time, remember? Mao Zedong and Karamatsov were sick, twisted bastards that wanted only power and position."

Delervello held up a hand. "I am not promoting Mao, Dr. Rourke. But I am raising a question on the survival of the KGB Elite Corp."

John nodded. "You're saying if we did... they could have."

"Exactly," Delervello said, smiling, "and if that is true it would be a logical next step to assume they are either still aligned with the Aliens and might well in fact be aligned with the KI."

Chapter Eighty-Seven

The die was set, the game had been set in motion and there was nothing left to do except play the hand out. Michael sat at his desk in the Presidential office. In front of it, technicians had set up lights and a movie camera on a tripod. A microphone keyed to the camera sat on the desk in front of him. He took a deep breath and nodded to Natalia. She pushed the start switch and signaled Michael to begin.

"My fellow Americans... The attacks on and against my father are attacks against you. We are being used as an excuse for changes that do not need to be and should not be made. We are being used as a reason by which your rights, your freedoms along with ours shall be removed. That is unacceptable. Already there is a call for our arrests, and calls for us to be branded outlaws, rogues and even brigands. Some of those voices are even coming from members of my administration. We are—you are— entering into a time of confusion, platitudes and misinformation. My father has told me of times in the past when these sort of things occurred. When the lure of personal gain, personal finances and or personal power took a higher precedence than personal honor and public duty, good men make bad choices.

"I have always distrusted many of our politicians; I now distrust the political process. It is flawed; it has been flawed for a long time and it will remain flawed because power is just too seductive.

"Today..." Michael laid down his notes and looked directly into the camera. "Today, many citizens no longer believe in politicians or the government. The pitiful thing is neither side is particularly concerned about it. The power, the prestige has blinded the government and the citizens are numb to the disgust they themselves feel. It is as if a blanket of malaise has been spread across the country. Individual politicians are neither astonished by such claims nor admit it but blame it on the other party.

"Our labor unions dismiss it as some form of radicalism; they no longer give a damn about the lives and fortunes of their members. They instead have become the very thing they were founded to stop... uncaring unprincipled politicians more concerned about themselves and their 'legacy,' more concerned about keeping the 'coffers full of membership dues' than anything else.

"From time to time, I believe the founding fathers realized the saying 'the only thing worse than a bad government is no government,' simply was not true. They realized that man is flawed and sometimes men must protect themselves against the very ones they have appointed to manage their national affairs.

"Our own Declaration of Independence took note of this: *'But when a long train of abuses and usurpations, pursuing invariably the same Object, evinces a design to reduce them under absolute Despotism, it is their right, it is their duty, to throw off such Government, and to provide new Guards for their future security.'*

"As bad as I hate to say it, it is time for this country—even the world— to shake itself again and throw off the fleas of greed, despotism and dishonesty. The reasons for distrust, the elements of lies and the planks of corruption— dishonesty, manipulation—the offenses perpetrated by our leaders from both parties have finally reached a critical mass. Our politicians now routinely dodge and side step and change every promise made simply to maintain the most dysfunctional and corrupt form of government possible—for their own benefit and the benefit of their corrupt handlers.

"Those people behind the scenes that are dedicated to the most perverse forms of contemptible circumstances for a so-called 'World view, a greater common good'... or whatever other form of nonsensical, hyperbole they can utter.

"Whether an investigation by law enforcement or Congress—whether that report is made by testimony, notarized statement or witnessed oral statements— once in office, neither party is particularly inclined to tell the truth any more. Now, it is perfectly acceptable for the government and the media to knowingly deceive contradict or lie to the citizens. It is time that the individual citizen must throw off the shackles of political correctness, the ropes of political corruption and cronyism and hypocrisy.

"I wish I could promise you success for such actions. I cannot. By its very nature, government is necessary to manage the needs of large numbers of similarly minded individuals. The very fact that God Almighty gave us free determination means our similarity in thought, mission and consideration is at best... short lived and corruptible.

"And this corruptibility is masked under fine sounded, seductive concepts like 'those with more need to share with those who have less' and 'From each according to his ability, to each according to his need.' Probably the most famous mystical, magical, mythical 'obligation of fairness' the world has ever heard.

"By the time you hear this message I will have resigned as your President. I will have removed my family from the grasping hands of those that would attack us. You see, I have made my decision.

"Edward Everett Hale, an American author and Unitarian clergyman, once said, 'I am only one, but still I am one. I cannot do everything, but still I can do something; and because I cannot do everything, I will not refuse to do the something that I can do.'

I have determined that the best way to serve my country is to serve my family first. I suggest the same is true for each of you.

"One day, and I hope it is soon... I pray to see America truly become the United States again. I pray to see good men strive hard to serve their country and freedom and responsibility reign again in this country. I pray to see the American eagle rise again like a Phoenix, rising from the ashes of its old self to the glory of its new life.

"We will meet again but not until the Rourke family has handled some challenges only we can handle. Until then, guard your dreams; guard your family and Plan Ahead."

Chapter Eighty-Eight

Rourke and The Keeper had visited on the quandary of how to get The Captain to "spill the beans" on his alignment with the Russians. Certainly, the Russian presence onboard several KI ships spoke of the alliance but did not identify the real reason for it. That was, the destruction of freedom throughout the world and the establishment of the New World Order with the survivors of Karamatsov's Elite KGB Guard at the helm.

The Keeper had returned to the armada, he had coordinated with the Seneia and the plan was well in place. Telepathically, he contacted John.

In his mind, Rourke heard The Keeper speak, *We, the Seneia of the KI, are the eldest of our people. We are the only ones that still practice the disciplines involved in mind to mind contact.*

Long before the eldest of us was born, our people had restricted this mind to mind contact from the general population. All KI have this ability, but not the knowledge of how to access it. Even your people have it, but your abilities are even more limited than that of my people. Once, what your people call Extrasensory Perception was a normal part of our ancestor's lives and not considered extra.

For us, Extrasensory Perception, or ESP, refers to perceptions gained through the mind, rather than through the traditional five recognized senses. We shall be counting on an individual's ability to predict an outcome of events by judging current circumstances. We shall simply be projecting a view of the current circumstances of our own invention through telepathy.

As you are aware, telepathy is the ability to communicate with one or more persons using only their mind and no other sensory input. But it also is the ability to gain limited control on certain motor and cognitive sections of another person's mind. It is somewhat like hypnosis, in that a person will not do something they would not normally do. We are able to alter a person's perception of reality and create a circumstance that fits their moral and ethical persuasions and allow for them to 'do what we wish them to do.'

Through a form of clairvoyance and clairaudience we are able to see objects or events and hear objects or events that are happening to someone else and then transmit those sights and sounds to another person, thereby changing their perception of reality. This is enhanced by a form of clairsentience; the ability to perceive a feeling throughout the whole body and transmit that feeling.

Like an empath? John asked.

Similar but not the same, the empathic person receives the perception of a feeling but cannot transmit it to others.

Is the person you are transmitting to aware of what you are doing?

In this case, he cannot be aware of what we are doing. We have to create what you would call a Trojan horse. Something that is not what it seems in order to elicit a response the person would not normally respond with. We must make a person deviate from normal linear thinking but do it in such a manner that it is not identified as a mental aberration.

Tell the truth, John. Simply tell the truth.

Chapter Eighty-Nine

In the end, after John Rourke's testimony, The Captain was led into the dark room. Seated on a dais was The Seneia of the KI, scholars and philosophers who held the greatest knowledge of the KI. The Seneia was the strength of the entire society, and now shared in its shame.

One of the Seneia began repeating a single word, "Kathaírō... Kathaírō..." Others began to join in and soon there was a chant that grew louder and louder. "Kathaírō... Kathaírō... Kathaírō, Kathaírō... Kathaírō... Kathaírō, Kathaírō... Kathaírō... Kathaírō, Kathaírō... Kathaírō... Kathaírō."

The Keeper raised one hand and stood, the chanting stopped.

"We must begin. We must once again return that which is unclean to cleanness. We must correct the wrong mixture, that which is broken must be made unbroken... that which is unclean must be made clean again and that tainted by sin must become untainted. IT must be made whole again and fruitful once more through purification. To do this, we must see what cannot be seen, touch that which cannot be touched, hear what cannot be heard and feel that which does not exist. We must know the unknowable and think the unthinkable in order to attain the unattainable.

"Captain, you have lied; something that has been the greatest sin in the KI culture... until now. You sought to be more than those that created you. You desired to reap a harvest you never planted, to take a profit you never earned and to win honors you never deserved. You turned your back on a world that had been given to you. You turned your back on a sun that warmed you. You turned your back on an ocean that bathed you. You turned your back on all that was for you and in the turning you took your people with you.

"From them you stole their land; from them you stole their world, their science, their peace and their honor. You exchanged their lives for an existence inside these metal wombs. You doomed some of your own people to death in the most horrendous ways and stranded others on a world that had gone mad and was destroying itself. You sought glory and found only legends, legends that you yourself never heard. Why? In the process you have left everything that once was you and have found nothing that should be you.

"Now inside this metal tube, you shall be launched into the darkness that you took your own people. You are not in control of its flight any more than your people were in control of theirs. You will fly through the darkness as we did; only glimpsing suns and never feeling their warmth. As we were, you are only a passenger now. You have no control of this ship, no control of your destiny. The only difference is you will have no companions except your own greed and selfishness.

"You shall travel at a speed that will be maintained until the heavens turn to ashes, an unknown speck in eternal darkness, insignificant to time and space. No one shall have mercy on your cold dark soul, you are dead to us. Your name shall be stricken from the rolls of KI. Your name shall not be spoken. Would that we could erase even the memory of you... we would. You are dead to us."

While The Keeper was speaking, The Captain was lead to his container. All military rank was ripped from his uniform. His normal poise was gone. His eyes like that those of a trapped animal flashed from side to side to seek a way to escape. There was no way out, he began to fight.

The Keeper had disgust in his voice. "Captain, do you not have enough bravery left, enough honor left to meet your fate correctly?"

The Captain's voice quivered, "I... I am sorry. I was wrong, what I did was wrong." He was buckled into the cylinder. "I am sorry, please... please, give me another..." Clank! The lid to the cylinder was dropped into place and locked. Through the view port, his face... a face that now showed nothing but fear with a trace of madness in it.

The Keeper asked, "Have the coordinates been entered?"

"They have," some technician said.

"Then, be done with this event."

The cylinder was picked by a small crane and placed into a chute. The belt at the bottom of the chute began to move toward a portal in the side of the ship. A hatch opened and the cylinder went inside and the hatch was closed.

Inside the ship a loud WHOOOSH was heard. Outside of the ship there was nothing but the silence of space. The Seneia of the KI reached out with their minds and made contact with the mind of the Captain. They heard, "PLEASE, PLEASE, PLEASE..."

The Captain heard them, "Kathaírō... Kathaírō... Kathaírō, Kathaírō... Kathaírō... Kathaírō, Kathaírō... Kathaírō... Kathaírō, Kathaírō... Kathaírō... Kathaírō." The sound in his mind was beautiful, the most beautiful and wonderful thing he had ever heard. He was not alone. But in just moments he noticed the Kathaírō... Kathaírō... Kathaírō, Kathaírō... Kathaírō... Kathaírō, Kathaírō... Kathaírō... Kathaírō, Kathaírō... Kathaírō... Kathaírō" was becoming quieter.

Members of the Seneia were no longer chanting, soon the magnificent cacophony of voices was down to just a few... then just two... and finally The Keeper stopped. He said, "You are dead to us."

The Captain screamed again and again and again...and again.

Chapter Ninety

Air Force Chief of Staff, General Frank Sullivan looked up as a knock sounded on his office door. Before he could say "Come in" the door opened. His secretary, Helen Bates, leaned in and said, "General, turn on your television." The look on her face and intensity of her voice silenced any retort on Sullivan's face. He found the remote and punched a button.

Banners of NEWS ALERT flashed across the screen as lead-in music blared. From off camera a sheet of paper was handed to the news anchor, a pretty blonde with perfect hair and gorgeous figure, who sat for a moment reading it, cleared her throat, took a deep breath and said, "Eyewitness News brings you a developing news story... Ladies and Gentlemen, satellite feeds are showing a series of massive explosions in space. At first reports, these explosions appear to be in close proximity to the location of the KI Armada centered above the South Pole at a distance of 600 miles above the earth's surface."

Sullivan reached for his intercom, punched a button and said, "Get your ass up here and bring all the data you have. Why am I finding out about this from the damn news media?" He slammed the phone down and said to Helen, "Get the President on the phone, call a meeting of the Joint Chiefs and..."

Helen was pushed out of the doorway from behind; a figure pushed passed her and stared at Sullivan.

"It is true then," Sullivan said.

The Keeper nodded. "I am afraid so, General. Something terrible has happened. Something terrible..." The Keeper leaned against Helen as Sullivan jumped to his feet. Grabbing The Keeper, Sullivan supported the older man's entire body weight and eased him in to a chair.

"Find John Rourke... Find him quickly General, there is not much time."

Chapter Ninety-One

Paul and Annie were the last to arrive at the secluded Presidential retreat on the eastern tip of Maui. The beautiful white sand beach was lapped by gentle waves and the sun began to drop in the afternoon sky. The weather was cool, almost brisk and heavy clouds were moving toward the island. The main house, a large single story ranch type affair with two verandas and an Olympic size swimming pool, stood on a well-manicured lawn. With eight bedrooms, ten full baths, a large library and a study, the house boasted nearly 9,000 square feet and that did not include the four car garage.

The household staff had been released and sent home. This was a private function. It was October, time for a Rourke family tradition; the celebration of the birthday of Natalia's uncle, General Ishmael Varakov, leader of the Soviet Occupation Forces in America immediately after The Night of the War.

Though the enemy of America, many times Varakov had proven himself to be a patriotic, honorable and reasonable Soviet soldier, and John Thomas Rourke appreciated that the Russian had helped him stop some of the more extreme plans of the KGB.

Over the years, it had not always been possible to have a celebration... many times the event was reduced to simply a remembrance. A few moments stolen from the reality of a world that had gone insane. However, the birthday was remembered... it was always a special heartwarming and heart breaking time for Natalia, his much beloved niece.

John Rourke retold the last conversation he and Varakov had. "I told him that, 'We could have been friends if all of us hadn't been so bent on butchering each other, Sir.' He responded, 'I think that you are quite correct, Dr. Rourke.' Varakov motioned toward Natalia, and said to me, 'You will care for her... I trust you and you alone with the greatest joy of my life,' Varakov said. Then he said, 'We communists are taught that there is no God to believe in... but in the event we have been wrong all these decades since we attempted to liberate man from his chains, then I wish that God, if He exists, will bless you all and protect you.' I told him, 'We capitalists are taught that hedging your bet is never a bad thing, General. May God bless you, too.'"

Natalia sniffled back a tear and said, "Then he folded me into his arms, and in Russian had said, 'I love you, you are the daughter, you are the life I never led. Kiss me goodbye, child... forever.' And I did."

Tears rolled down Natalia's cheeks as they always did when this story was told.

Now, a tradition that began after Michael and Natalia had married, began. Over the years a closing toast had become part of the festivities; it was a paraphrase of the last words John and Natalia heard spoken by General Ishmael Varakov, leader of the Soviet Occupation Forces in America. Michael had not known Varakov or heard the Old Russian speak, but his father had made certain that Varakov and his last words would never be forgotten, at least not by a Rourke.

Michael charged each glass with Champagne. This year Paula, John and Emma's daughter, and Natalie, Paul and Annie's daughter would imbibe for the first time.

"Everyone's glasses charged?" Michael asked. Raising his glass in salute, he said, "To General Ishmael Varakov, honored soldier, loving uncle and valued friend... May, 'God, if He hears me and if He is there to begin with, grant you God speed. Happy Birthday."

The ceremony was a short one, and everyone adjourned to the veranda where steaks sizzled on the outdoor cook stove. John walked up to Michael. "Everything ready?"

Michael nodded. "Yep, and the steaks are also."

After the meal, the children went down to the beach and played while the adults sat around on the veranda visiting. Annie squeezed Paul's hand and said with a smile, "This was one of the best birthday parties Uncle Ishmael ever had."

Chapter Ninety-Two

It was shortly after 11:00p.m.when the first sirens broke the still night. Police cars, fire trucks and ambulances sped toward the eastern tip of Maui and the Presidential Retreat.

Guards at the entry control points waved them through the gates with urgency. Before the last curve of the driveway was negotiated, the first responders knew it was useless. Fires blazed in a half a dozen locations. The quiet scene had been shattered by an explosion so massive the walls of the main house disappeared into a cloud of shrapnel moving outward at an incredible rate of speed. Sections of the roof had been blown high into the air, broken by the concussion and flung into the neighboring jungle creating the fires.

The main house... the main house and the four car garage simply did not exist any longer. Parts of furniture and clothing smoldered around the grounds. The four vehicles that had brought the Rourke family to the main house had been tossed like toys; now their shattered skeletons burned brightly in the dark as their interiors were consumed.

The on-scene commander muttered, "Mother of God," as he dismounted the Command Support Unit. "Get the pump ladder on the house. Make sure the gas is turned off; we don't want to cook off another explosion. Send the turntable ladders to start killing the jungle fires before we have more of a mess." He stopped to survey the disaster scene again. "I want the Rescue Company, and the Tanker Trucks to knock out the rest of the structure fire. Send the Foam Tenders to put out the grass fires. I don't want evidence washed away if there is any evidence in the yard."

"What about the ambulances?" Somebody asked.

"Keep them back from the scene and out of the way."

"But, but the President... The Rourkes..."

The on-scene commander wheeled, "No one survived this blast, damnit Lieutenant... No one. This is not going to be a rescue mission but a recovery one. Looks to me like a gas explosion, even the foundation of the structure is gone, nothing but a crater. We're not going to find bodies... we're going to find pieces of bodies and that is if we're damned lucky."

"I can't believe it, the President and First Lady... the entire Rourke family dead. I can't believe it. To have survived all they have survived and to die like this, in an accidental explosion..."

Chapter Ninety-Three

It was time; Phillip Greene adjusted his tie in the mirror. His frumpy wife, Marilyn, was in an expensive but rather gauche outfit that did nothing for her figure. Her attitude rather matched her outfit he thought.

"Hurry up, Phillip. I don't want to be late. Why does the inauguration have to be today? The weather is not going to make my hair do well, the humidity is terrible." Greene ignored her as he usually did.

Phillip Greene was about to be made President of the United States of America after all. He wiped at the drool that still dripped from the left side of his jaw. Doctors had told him there was nerve damage that might take months to heal. It never had. Luckily, its effect on his speech had been limited. He smiled, the permanent replacement dental appliances, namely six false teeth to replace the ones Rourke had knocked out during their first debate, shown white and straight.

He stopped for a moment and looked in the mirror. *It's really going to happen,* he thought. *After all of this time, it is really going to happen. Michael Rourke, hell the whole Rourke family gone. I'm going to be the President.* His cell phone chirped on the chest of drawers. *Oh, crap,* he thought seeing the caller ID.

"Congratulations, Mr. President." Peter Vale's voice was as smooth as honey.

"Well, not yet, hahaha. Not until the inauguration, not for another hour." He wondered how this man had the ability to shake his confidence to the point of distraction.

"Yes, Mr. Greene, you are correct but I wanted to congratulate you myself. It will be a real pleasure working with your administration. We will make things different, won't we Mr. Greene?"

"Hahaha, yes... different. Better don't you think? *I am shaking like a cat in the top of a tree. How does this man do this to me? Hell... I'm the President of the United States.*

"Well again, Sir, congratulations and enjoy the festivities. I will see you in your office tomorrow morning."

Greene gripped the phone tightly. *I've got to get control of this right now or I never will. I have to show Vale who he is dealing with. I have to make my stand and position clear.* That was what he thought, what he said was, "Certainly, until tomorrow." Greene would never understand how Vale had made this happen. Congress itself had voted unanimously to bypass procedure and protocol and the electoral process and simply appoint Phillip Greene to be the next President of the United States.

*****

His wife babbled and waved at people through the car window; she was having the time of her life. Phillip Greene sat in the back of the limousine, lost in thought. *Everyone says it was an accident. I've seen the reports that said it was a gas leak; old faulty piping under the Presidential Retreat that finally gave way. It leaked out, found a pocket and enough finally collected that when the explosion happened... everything was destroyed and everybody was vaporized.* He shuddered.

Was it an accident or did Vale actually have the President and his family killed? Will I ever know; does it even matter? As long as I keep Vale happy, Vale will keep me happy. Really, it is really that simple isn't it? Of course it is. This is what I've wanted; now I have made it.

*****

The head of the Presidential Security Detail, Frank Zimmerman was disgusted and nervous; disgusted that he was on this detail and nervous because it should not have been necessary. Michael Rourke should still be the president.

Having said that, at least in his own mind, Zimmerman refocused; it was his responsibility to put a wall of protection around the man about to be made President of the United States. Zimmerman looked older than his late forties and haggard, the past days had aged him. He liked Michael Rourke. He liked the whole family.

Zimmerman looked around the venue, scattered throughout the crowd were his twenty-seven dedicated agents, their sole purposes—protect the President and prevent any "unplanned events." His guys were the best expert shots and trained in hand-to-hand, each one a specially trained and hand-picked professional; each ready at a moment's notice to whisk the President away to safety.

Zimmerman shook his head, *Now we've got just another politician to protect. He'll never be the man Michael Rourke was. I just have to stay focused, stay alert and for God's sake stay in communication. By this time tomorrow, we will have a new President, just not much of one.*

Chapter Ninety-Four

The satellite feed focused on the cluster of KI ships in geo-synchronous or-bit approximately 200 miles from the surface of Earth. Depending on your perspective it was either directly above or directly below the continent of Antarctica. It had been focused on that formation since the KI fleet positioned itself there upon their return to Earth. In all that time, there had only been two changes. One, two months ago, there had been a short interruption of the feed that lasted fifteen seconds. It had been blamed on a possible solar flare or power surge.

The second, yesterday, with three of the ships appearing to explode.

At first, the movement in the KI armada had almost been missed altogether. Then it became more and more apparent. The ships were moving further and further apart and into a different formation. Then small glints of reflected light began to emerge from the KI ships, the lights coalesced into five separate formations.

Four formations began a dive toward the atmosphere, the fifth and smallest of the formations took up a position away from the rest of the fleet and waited. Fifteen seconds later the four formations diving toward the atmosphere were out of sight of the satellite's camera.

The claxon sounded at the Air Command Headquarters and at every military installation in the world. Scores of alert aircraft leapt into the skies above southern Europe, surface to air missiles flew out of launch control facilities and off the racks of mobile launchers from the continental U.S. and Hawaii. Strangely no response to the threat came from New Germany or South America. Likewise, Australia and the western Pacific was quiet.

But from Asia, several flights of Russian fighter planes, the Mikoyan MiG-122 and MiG-122Ds climbed into the sky. They weren't there to combat the KI threat... they were there to support it. The MiG-122, a multi-role fighter plane is a single-seat version, with improved avionics and weapons systems and preci-sion-guided targeting capability. The two-seater is known as the MiG-122 D.

Six fighters from Mid-Wake met the Russian and KI formation one hundred miles off the southeast coast of Japan. Outnumbered over three to one, the Mid-Wake fighters still dropped four Russian MiGs and one of the KI before being blown out of the sky. The first engagement of the new war, The Battle of the Sea of Japan, went to the enemy.

Planes from Honolulu and the continental U.S. never launched. That order came from the President of the United States himself; Philip Green. Effectively, the United States of America, New Germany and Australia had been taken out of the fight politically. The air forces of England and Spain were decimated within minutes. The KI technology was more advanced than anything those pilots had ever encountered.

Apparently one thing that the KI craft, or their pilots, could not contend with was massive atmospheric disturbances with lightning. The KI formation assigned to the continental U.S. disappeared in such a disturbance over the Alaskan coast line, with no survivors.

*****

The satellite phone chirped in Frank Sullivan's brief case. He pulled to the side of the road and stopped. Setting the briefcase on the seat, he thumbed the latches and pulled out the phone. There was a text message on the screen; a single word—Marco.

Epilogue

The resignation tape Michael Rourke made that day in his office was never seen by the public. According to a story released by Agnes Briggs, World Associate Press, that tape was seized from the offices of DOT —Dead on Target —Television News after Bill Nolan, Senior Commentator for DOT, announced that he had come into possession of the tape.

"It was 'supposedly' seized on the direct orders of the new President of the United States, Phillip Greene; a claim that has not been substantiated. It should be noted that Mr. Nolan was also taken into custody on unspecified charges pending an investigation. Mr. Nolan was last seen being removed from DOT Headquarters shouting he was innocent of all charges. To date, Mr. Nolan's condition and whereabouts have not been released by authorities."

In her weekly column, Ms. Briggs reported that in several unrelated stories some members of the Rourke administration have had their offices searched by Federal authorities and some have been arrested on charges of sedition, malfeasance and corruption. In a staggering move, all Army and Air National Guard Units have been federalized and ordered by the President to active duty either in their reserve component status or by calling them into Federal service in their militia status.

And shortly after the Guard was federalized, the Posse Comitatus Act was declared null and void by the Supreme Court. That Act, part of 18 United States Code had been in effect since it was signed on June 18, 1878 by President Rutherford B. Hayes. In concert with the Insurrection Act of 1807, Posse Comitatus limited the powers of the government in using military personnel to enforce domestic policies within the United States.

In an unusual but not unheard of move, President Greene announced the appointment of Mr. Peter Vale as ambassador-at-large. The ambassador-at-large is a diplomat of the highest rank who is accredited to represent his country and people internationally. Unlike an ambassador-in-residence who is usually limited to a country or embassy, the ambassador-at-large is entrusted to operate in several countries or regions or sometimes hold a seat in international organization. Historically, presidents or prime ministers have designated special diplomatic envoys for specific assignments, primarily overseas but sometimes also within the country as an ambassador-at-large. President Greene's first thirteen days in office has been extremely active.

The extermination of the genetically modified VBB, Very Bad Bug, has been an extreme success with the World Health Organization declaring the Hanta Virus epidemic, spread by the insect, has been neutralized. There has still been no report on where or how the VBB made an appearance.

Ms. Briggs admitted that the only dark spot on the horizon for President Greene administration has been the unexplained loss of several military aircraft; presumably due to accidents. President Greene has stated for the record that, "These terrible accidents and losses of life fall unfortunately on the desk of my predecessor, President Michael Rourke who took no steps whatsoever to upgrade our military equipment or personnel. To date, five Vertical Take Off and Landing transports and their crews have been lost in training missions over the Pacific Ocean.

"Unfortunately, our naval forces have been unable to locate the crash sites, debris or survivors. All of these missions have moved from the Rescue Phase to recovery of our lost service members, none of whom have been located."

Ms. Briggs also reported that meetings have taken place with representatives of the New National Socialist Faction of the Democratic German Republic. This worthwhile organization is leading the way in developing countries across the globe. Newly established Factions are now functioning in all of the major nations of the world with hopes to have a branch developed in the United States, soon.

President Greene scoffed at rumors that this organization is a front for some type of New World Order. "That is total nonsense and that type of reporting is nothing but scare tactics that stem from fears and rumors and tactics that go back to the 20th Century and The Night Before the War. Our culture is an advanced one, we have made advances and we have more to make. We can no longer be hobbled by the 'boogie man' legends associated with the past. Frankly, if a New World Order was capable of improving the human condition globally... that doesn't sound like a bad idea to me. I have instructed our ambassador-at-large, Ambassador Vale to work diligently on developing goals for the approaching millennium."

President Greene said he would like to see goals such as: Ending poverty in all its forms everywhere. Ending hunger, achieve food security and improved nutrition and promote sustainable agriculture. Ensuring healthy lives and promoting well-being for all at all ages. Ensuring inclusive and equitable quality education and promote lifelong learning opportunities for all. Achieving true gender equality and empower all women and girls. Developing and having available and sustainable management of water and sanitation for all. "We must develop affordable, reliable, sustainable modern energy for everyone." President Greene added, "These are just of few of the areas that I think Mankind is ready for and Ambassador Vale will be working on.

Ms. Briggs also reported that the Mexican news agency, El Periódico Nacional, has published unsubstantiated stories of increased UFO activity across the globe. Representatives of the KI deny any of their craft have been involved and our own government has reversed its position on UFOs with the following statement. "Unfortunately, earlier reports of unexplained flying object activity were either grossly over reported or simply fabricated. It is regretful that members of the military and civilian population gave vent to wild stories such as the terrible events involved with major destruction in Honolulu on the occasion of President Rourke's inauguration, involved UFOs. The National Transportation Safety Board, recently amended his report of that incident citing "confusion and massive debris distribution from the crash of an airliner resulted in the misidentification of unidentified flying debris."

She closed her report with this admonition, "It boggles my mind that in this advanced age there remains such a fascination with flying saucers. Let's grow up, people."

*****

"As the crow flies", it is about 3,973 miles from Honolulu to what is remaining of Springfield, Missouri.

Jerry Ahern, Sharon Ahern and Bob Anderson

About three miles from what is left of the control tower at the old Springfield Airport, a man stood. He watched as people rushed about with their duties, doing the things that needed to be done. He cuffed his Rolex Submariner and checked the time... it wouldn't be long now.

He removed his aviator sunglasses, wiping sweat away before replacing the glasses. He reached into his shirt pocket and pulled out a thin, dark cigar. From his watch pocket in his jeans, he pulled a battered Zippo lighter, with an emblem engraved on it.

He flipped the lid, rolled the striker wheel creating a yellow blue flame. He puffed a couple of times to get it going and snapped the lid shut and put the lighter back in his pocket. From a chair next to him, he picked up the double Alessi holster that held twin stainless Detonics CombatMasters and put his arms through the straps. He shrugged slightly to settle the rig and he patted the left rear side of his belt, feeling for the A.G. Russell Survivalist Sting.

He put on the battered brown leather bomber jacket and slung a musette bag over one shoulder. He was ready. He was John Thomas Rourke and he would survive.

On Sale Now!

The Survivalist *series*

On Sale Now!

CAMP ZERO series is based on characters created by
*Jerry Ahern, Sharon Ahern and Bob Anderson in
The Survivalist series.*

**For more information
visit:** www.speakingvolumes.us

On Sale Now!

Surgical Strike *series*

On Sale Now!

The Defender *series*

For more information
visit: www.speakingvolumes.us

On Sale Now!

They Call Me the Mercenary *series*
Axel Kilgore (Jerry Ahern)

For more information
visit: www.speakingvolumes.us

Sign up for free and bargain books

Join the Speaking Volumes mailing list

Text
ILOVEBOOKS
to 22828 to get started.

Message and data rates may apply